VODKA CALIPHATE

Lee A. Sweetapple

This is a work of fiction. All characters, names, incidents, organizations, and dialogue in this novel is either the product of the author's imagination or is used fictitiously.

© 2017 Lee A. Sweetapple
ISBN: 0692931538
ISBN-13: 9780692931530
Library of Congress Control Number: 2017951298
Eclectic Manor Publishing, Marshall, VA

This book is dedicated to the scientists who go to the dangerous corners of the globe to explore our world and help us understand our interdependencies.

ACKNOWLEDGMENTS

Thank you, Lyn, for your love and your incremental editing as I waded through this long process. Thank you, Arnold S., for exposing me to diving for science instead of only for adventure.

CHAPTER 1

SÃO TOMÉ
06 0945 JULY

Dr. Gwen Stillwater and Dr. Tanya Melnik made last-minute checks of their scuba gear as the dive boat slowed and the mate threw the anchor over the side. Tanks full and secure, regulators tested, they took one last swig of water. The two women were about to dive on one of the most pristine coral reefs in the world, located just off the west coast of Africa.

"It makes me cringe every time they throw an anchor onto the reef instead of tying off on a buoy. There goes another big chunk of staghorn coral," Gwen said as she zipped her Lycra stinger suit and pulled her scuba mask up over her face.

"I know what you mean, but who's going to pay for a buoy for them to tie off on?" Tanya replied before she stuck her regulator in her mouth and moved back toward the dive platform.

Gwen noticed that Tanya always seemed to be in a hurry to get in the water when they got to a dive site and suspected that she was hiding a mild case of seasickness. Her nausea could quickly grow worse without the breeze from the moving boat on this ninety-two-degree day, especially with the new rolling motion of the boat as it now bobbed on the end of the anchor line in two- to three-foot seas.

The captain gave a thumbs-up from the wheelhouse of the boat, and Michael, the mate, rushed to the back of the boat to first throw in a tag line with a float at the end and then help Tanya and Gwen into the water.

Gwen smiled as she watched the petite young São Toméan mate seem to almost dance as he moved around on the deck of the dive boat. He could barely keep his eyes off Gwen and Tanya as he moved about. Both women were lean and athletic. Tanya looked like a basketball player, tall, with long white-blond hair. Her arms were sculptured, but not from basketballs, instead from sabers, foils, and heavy draw longbows. Gwen was built more like a swimmer, only a little above average height, and with strong shoulders that met her wheat-blond hair.

Tanya followed the tag line into the water and remained buoyant while holding on to the tag line until Gwen joined her in the water. The seventy-eight-degree water seemed cool compared to the hot equatorial sun. The two divers flashed the OK sign to each other, lifted the dump valves over their heads, and released some air from the buoyancy compensators to start their descent to the coral reef thirty-five feet below. The two divers slowed their descent as they neared the coral reef and hovered several feet above some fan and brain coral.

As soon as they had dropped down to their working depth and stabilized their buoyancy, both Gwen and Tanya checked their gauges. Air pressure was good, and depth was just under thirty feet, which meant that how fast they went through their air would be the only limiting factor on their dive. Gwen and Tanya were both in excellent shape and comfortable with diving, so barring any unexpected excitement, their dive could easily last more than an hour.

Visibility was still good at more than a hundred feet, and the vibrant colors of the reef produced smiles in the eyes of both divers. The reef seemed healthy, heavily populated with feeder fish, blacktip reef sharks, schools of barracuda and tuna. Gwen and Tanya paused to watch a manta ray swim past them. The diversity of fish they saw in just the first few minutes of their dive delighted the two scientists. Tanya raised her Nikonos underwater camera and took a quick picture of Gwen, trying to catch the manta ray in the frame, as Gwen double-checked that her collection bags were still zipped shut.

Gwen pulled out a tape measure and checked the diameter of the brain coral while Tanya took a few more shots of Gwen and the big coral formation with her camera. The two spent the next ten minutes moving along the top of the reef, distracted only for a moment by a curious large shark that had likely heard them splash into the water. As they swam over a slight mound, the bright colors of the reef were replaced by a dull black-and-brown landscape. It looked like a considerable section of the reef had been spray-painted with used motor oil and tar. Gwen pulled out her dive knife and used it to scrape some of the substance into one of her Nalgene collection bottles. Gwen frowned as she noticed that she had stained the arm of her new bright-blue stinger suit with the substance that she was fairly certain was some form of oil. Tanya continued to photograph Gwen's progress as the other woman moved to where the substance coating the reef seemed to be a lighter shade of brown. In other areas, the coral seemed to be undergoing bleaching.

As Gwen and Tanya continued to move across the reef, exploring the extent of the damage, they turned and looked first at each

3

other and then up when the distinctive high-pitched sound of several outboard boat motors became louder and then slowed. *They probably saw our dive flag*, Gwen thought.

Tanya pointed at her watch and then pointed back in the direction they had come from, and Gwen knew that it was time to start moving back toward the dive boat. In another ten minutes, they were near where they had entered the water. Both divers were puzzled when the dive boat's engine started and their ride began to move away. The high-pitched sound of outboard motors was suddenly loud again, but the sound soon diminished as these boats moved away too.

Gwen and Tanya exchanged a look of horror, and both women started their slow ascent to see what was going on while they became increasingly worried about being hit by one of the boats on the surface.

Tanya broke the surface first and inflated her BC after doing a hasty 360 to check for any boats. "What the hell!" she exclaimed as she watched their dive boat drive away at full speed, chased by two large dhows.

Gwen popped up next to Tanya and quickly realized what had happened.

"Well, Jim did warn us about pirates," Gwen said with an incredulous tone. "Of course, I thought he was exaggerating. So what do we do now? We're more that fifteen miles from shore."

"I guess we start swimming. And hope that our dive boat got out a call for help. São Tomé does have a coast guard," Tanya reminded Gwen as she flipped over onto her back and started kicking, with her head pointed toward what was her best guess at the shortest route to land.

Gwen kicked her way next to Tanya.

"Hey, look, there's the float from the tag line. They must have been in too much of a hurry to pull it in, so they just cut it loose," Gwen said, pointing off to the side, and then changed her direction to swim toward the bright-orange float.

"What do you want that thing for?" Tanya asked, puzzled.

"We can use the line to hook ourselves together so we don't get separated after it gets dark," Gwen said as she grabbed hold of the float and started pulling on what turned out to be about twenty feet of nylon line. Gwen made a quick overhand knot about five feet from the float, leaving a loop that she clipped to her BC, and handed the other end of the line to Tanya for her to tie off on her BC.

"OK, all hooked up. That was a good idea," Tanya said as she flipped back over onto her back and started slowly kicking in the theoretical direction of land.

"Try not to splash," Gwen warned.

"I know. I saw the shark when we got into the water. It was at least fifteen feet long. Was it a great white?"

"No, I don't think so. It looked more like a mako," Gwen said as she continued her slow rhythmic kick cycle.

"I am so sorry I got you into this mess," Tanya said.

"Are you kidding? This was the opportunity of a lifetime. We'll get out of this OK—hopefully before Jim finds out, or he'll be getting the gang together for another adventure," Gwen answered as she smiled for the first time since they had surfaced.

"Another Jim Stillwater adventure? I guess I didn't see that one coming." Tanya laughed.

CHAPTER 2

FAIRFAX, VA
06 0930 JULY

Jim Stillwater, former US Army Intelligence Corps—mainly supporting special ops—and now a defense contractor, still maintained his military bearing as he walked into the office of the president of Symphonic Technology Partners, or STP. Only slightly taller than average, he looked like a typical soldier, his body formed from years of push-up, sit-ups, and running. His hair was dark brown and his green eyes made him even more in descript. He was the perfect build and coloring to blend in almost anywhere he went. With a good tan he blended well in the Middle East or South America, and without the dark tan he looked generically Northern European.

A coffee mug in hand, Jim gave a brief knock on the doorframe. Joe Golflink, Jim's boss, who was also a retired US Navy captain and ace fighter jock, had just gotten off the phone.

"Good morning, Jim. You'll be interested in this," Joe said, waving the other man into his office. "I just got a call from the 401(k) guys, and they will be rolling our money over from the buyout at the end of the month. No tax bill right now though, since all of our stock was in our retirement funds." He rose from behind a wooden A-4 Skyhawk on his large but overcrowded desk, and walked over to the big armchair next to a small wood coffee table and comfortable blue couch. In the early days of the company, Joe would often crash on the couch after working very late. "Have a seat. I have some time since I'm not really running this place anymore."

"Thanks, Joe. It's kind of a strange feeling to be part of such a big company after the buyout. How long do you think it will be until they get rid of the STP name and logo?"

"They won't fully integrate us until at least next year. I'll have moved on by then," Joe said before taking a sip of his coffee.

"Good chance that I'll be moving on too. Gwen wants me to take some time off before diving into the next start-up company."

"So how's Gwen doing? I can't believe that Tanya got that grant for the two of them to study the coral reef in São Tomé."

"I spoke with her yesterday. They were expecting good weather and planned to do their second dive today. She said that it was kind of funny that even though they were doing this survey prior to the new oil leases, it looked like there was already some significant hydrocarbon damage on the northern edge of the reef," Jim said as he plopped down on the couch across from Joe without spilling a drop of his coffee.

"So I get that Tanya works for the National Park Service now, but why are they paying for Gwen to go too?"

"The money is a UNESCO grant, and since Gwen is a trained marine biologist, she was an easy add to the grant. Tanya gets a trusted dive buddy this way too," Jim said as he sipped the still-steaming Café Bustelo.

"UN? OK, that makes sense, since it's one of those world biodiversity habitat things. Do they know that Tanya used to be a spook?" Joe asked with a wry smile.

"I'm guessing that she didn't bring that part up. It does make me feel better that she and Gwen are hanging out together. You saw what an ass-kicker Tanya is when LP was kidnapped by the drug dealers down in the Keys. I don't think I have ever seen anyone so comfortable in the Everglades either, unless they grew up down there," Jim said with a little bit of a smile as he remembered rescuing LP, deep in the Big Cypress Swamp National Preserve.

"So, is Tanya concerned about the pirates? There has been a lot of kidnapping in the Gulf of Guinea," Joe said, a creased brow now evident.

"I didn't mention that to Tanya. I did mention it to Gwen, but I don't think she was too worried. Most of the piracy was farther north, toward the oil rigs off the coast of Nigeria. It's not as bad as what's happening off Somalia, but I gotta admit I kind of have a bad feeling about this whole thing. She gets back next week though, and for once, Gwen will get to tell the war stories about an international adventure," Jim said with a mischievous smile.

"Well, if you need some time off and want to meet her somewhere after she's finished up the field work, take the days, Jim. This buyout crap has been taking up most of our time, and you have still been supporting your customer on top of that. Just think about it, OK?" Joe said as he stood up and moved back over behind his desk.

"OK, will do, Joe. I'll see if she wants to meet in Paris for a couple of days on her way back home. I'll talk to her tomorrow," Jim said as he got up and headed for the door.

Jim made a quick stop by the coffee bar and topped off his mug before making his way back down the hallway to the other corner office. *I wonder how long it'll be before the new owners get rid of the free coffee,* he thought, shaking his head.

Jim logged into his e-mail and looked for a note from Gwen saying that she was safely back on dry land. When he didn't find one, Jim guessed that she was too busy taking care of samples or had gone out with Tanya to enjoy the local food and music.

Jim was deep into a news article about Enterprise Aerospace's purchase of STP when he was startled by a knock on his open door. Jim looked up and smiled when he saw the tall athletic form of Morgan Smith, noting her long auburn hair draped over her silk blouse. She wore a tight leather skirt and six-inch heels. Morgan caught his glance and stepped forward into the office.

"Well, I know it's casual Friday, but I'm meeting some of the team for drinks after work, so no blue jeans for me today," Morgan explained as she twirled to show off her outfit.

"It looks great, Morgan. So, are you working on a scheme to form a new consulting company, perhaps?" Jim teased.

"Maybe. Why? Are you looking for employees?" Morgan replied, only half joking.

"I can't. I just signed a three-year noncompetition clause as part of my payout because the guys at EA expected me to do exactly that."

"Well, those of us with less stock than you didn't need to sign away our freedom." Morgan teased him too.

"I knew that this would happen eventually; I just didn't think it was going to be this soon. I hope you're not having second thoughts about leaving civil service," Jim said with a concerned look.

"Are you kidding me? This has been one of the best experiences ever, even with the craziness that went on in the Keys when LP got kidnapped and our escape from those rogue Mossad guys in Europe last year. Thanks to you and Joe, my professional network is broad enough now that if I decide to move, it will be to another fun place, like we used to have here. Or who knows? Maybe I'll go work in the wine-tasting room at LP's vineyard," Morgan said playfully, with a wink.

"So while we're not on the subject, have you heard any updates from Gwen? She must be having a blast." Morgan continued, a genuine and full smile returning to her face.

"She was diving today, so I expect a text when she is off the boat and probably a call from her tomorrow."

"Well, tell her that I said hello," Morgan said as she waved and then headed for the door.

"Will do, Morgan. Have a fun time this afternoon," Jim answered as he returned to his e-mail.

CHAPTER 3

SÃO TOMÉ
06 1100 JULY

Captain Rodrigues pushed forward on the throttle hard, just in case he could get a little bit more power from his big diesel inboard engines. He was slowly pulling away from the two dhows that were chasing him, but one or more men on the dhows were now shooting at his boat with what looked like AK-47s. One of the bullets hit the console beside him, and Captain Rodrigues ducked as shards of fiberglass from the boat zinged through the air.

"Get down below, and bring me my shotgun and a box of shells!" Rodrigues yelled at Michael. The young man scrambled down below as they continued to pull away from the dhows, heading in the direction of São Tomé. Rodrigues figured that they would be within radio range of the port soon, so he picked up the microphone, pressed the switch, and yelled, "Mayday! Mayday! This is *Sea Quest*, and we are under attack twelve miles north of Santo Antonio."

After waiting a moment for a reply, the captain repeated his call as Michael emerged from below with a stainless steel Mossberg twelve-gauge pump-action shotgun and a box of shells, apparently having no clue how to load the weapon.

"Here, take the wheel and give me the shotgun," the captain ordered.

The mate did as he was told and then ducked down low, fearing more bullets.

Captain Rodrigues quickly loaded the shotgun and fired three shots at the two dhows that were now more than fifty yards behind them. He doubted that he could hit them at that range on the bouncing boat, but after the third shot, the lead dhow turned sharply and broke off the chase. The second dhow followed suit, and both boats headed back in the direction they had come from.

"I think you hit them," Michael said excitedly. "What are you going to tell the police—that you killed some of the pirates?"

It suddenly sank in that the captain may have shot one of the pirates. Would they seek revenge? Would he need to defend his actions in court? "What pirates?" Captain Rodrigues asked with forced innocence. "This never happened. You let me do the talking and don't say a word, or you will never work on a boat in São Tomé again."

Gwen and Tanya continued their slow progress toward what they hoped was land. Gwen kept track of their heading with the small compass attached to her depth-gauge and submersible-pressure-gauge console, which she had pulled onto her belly so that the compass would be as close to level as possible.

"So how long do you think this will take?" Gwen asked as she looked over at Tanya and saw the look of grim determination on Tanya's face.

"Well, we're about twelve miles from shore. Most people can swim three to four miles an hour, but since we're going for the long haul here, let's say less than four hours," Tanya calculated.

"Yeah, but we have fins on and we're both strong swimmers, so maybe we can swim a little more than three to four miles an hour."

"OK, and wind is not a factor today. If there was a strong wind, we would really be screwed," Tanya said with a slight laugh.

"Yeah, as if we're not screwed enough as it is," Gwen said and chuckled.

"So if we are headed in the right direction, we could get to land in somewhere around three hours," Gwen concluded, a bit indecisively.

"We just need to keep this up, and if we don't see land in four or five hours, we can start to get concerned," Tanya said.

"Maybe. What worries me is the current. We have no land reference, and for all we know, we're going at three miles per hour against a five-mile-per-hour current."

"Yes, I did consider that too," Tanya said, "but I would like to think that maybe the current is working in our favor. We'll know if we see land in less than four hours or if we don't see land after five or six. So in the meantime, we just keep swimming." She surged ahead of Gwen with an extra kick for emphasis.

"So what's our plan if the dhows come back?" Gwen blurted out.

"Well, we don't have much air left, but I suppose we could submerge a few feet and wait until they go past," Tanya said slowly, unsure whether that was really a good idea.

"We don't know who the good guys are and who the bad guys are. I trusted the boat captain, but maybe he was in on this and planned to leave us out here," Gwen said as she continued her rhythmic kicks.

"I think we need to take advantage of any boats we see. We might be kicking against the current, and we don't have any fresh water. We are not going to last long like this," Tanya replied.

"I don't think we'll have to wait long to find out what's going on. Do you hear that?" Gwen looked off to her left in the direction of the sound of an outboard boat motor.

"You think they're pirates?" Tanya asked.

"Those are the right kind of boats. Good news is, Jim said that they almost always ransom off the people they kidnap without harming them. They see it as a good business practice."

"I think we're about to find out one way or another. There are two boats, and they both just turned and are now headed straight for us. Keep your dive knife handy. If they are kidnappers, maybe we can surprise them and steal their boat," Tanya said with a grim expression.

"You know I'll put up a fight," Gwen replied.

As the boats approached, Tanya unclipped from the tag line tether and clipped her nylon mesh collection bag to the line. She opened one of the ziplock bags inside the collection bag and used her black marker to write "2 X DHOWS" inside the plastic bag before she resealed it and placed it inside the collection bag.

"Gwen, unhook the tag line and let it go," Tanya yelled to Gwen.

Gwen unclipped and let the line go, and the float with Tanya's collection bag drifted away.

The two dhows slowed, having definitely spotted Tanya and Gwen, and pulled up on either side of them. Three very dark-skinned men were in one boat and four in the other. All of the men had AK-47s draped across their chests on slings. One man in each boat controlled a long tiller attached to the large outboard motors.

"Swim to the boats. We are here to rescue you," one of the men in the boat with four yelled out in a West African English accent. "Your captain left you here to die, but we are here to rescue you," he added.

Gwen and Tanya both swam toward the boat with the man who had called out to them.

"You, with the very long hair, come to this boat, and you over there, into the other boat," he yelled sharply, gesturing to Gwen with his open hand.

Gwen rolled over and kicked toward the other boat. The three men grabbed her BC under the armpits and lifted her, tank and all, completely out of the water and into the bottom of the boat almost effortlessly. Gwen looked over to see that two men were helping Tanya out of her dive gear.

"Some water for you?" One of the men who had lifted her out of the water handed Gwen a canteen.

Gwen nodded and took the water before looking around the boat, immediately noting that there was almost nothing in it besides gas cans and water jugs. *This is definitely not a fishing boat, and these guys are not São Toméan*, Gwen concluded silently.

The man who had offered her water yelled out in what Gwen recognized as an African coastal language, and the bow of the dhow rose as the craft accelerated and pulled up next to the one with Tanya in it. Gwen pulled off her flippers and struggled out of her BC, even shutting off the tank valve out of habit.

"Where are we going?" Gwen asked the same man.

"We are going to our village near Port Harcourt. You will be safe there. I am sure that your family will reward us for saving you from the ocean," the man said with a smile, revealing a gold upper front tooth.

Gwen frowned. "Why don't you take us to São Tomé?" she asked innocently.

"Because we are not supposed to be here—but lucky for you, we are." The man laughed. "I am Thomas," he said, placing his open hand over his chest. "So what is your name, lady with a frown?"

"My name is Gwen."

"Ah, I once knew a young lady named Gwendolyn."

"Name isn't Gwendolyn, just Gwen," Gwen corrected.

"OK, Just Gwen. Get some rest. We will not be to my home until very late tonight," Thomas said as he reached down to pull the dive knife out of the sheath attached to Gwen's leg. He held it away from her. "This is very sharp. I do not want you to hurt yourself with this," he said as he tossed the knife into a basket in the front of the dhow.

Gwen looked angrily at Thomas but didn't speak, and Thomas laughed for a moment and started a conversation with the man keeping lookout near the front of the dhow.

Thomas picked up what looked like a phone with a large antenna that almost had to be a SATCOM device this far from shore. He punched a long string of numbers into the keypad and placed it up to his ear. "Yes, this is Thomas. We have the two divers, but the boat got away." There was a pause. "Yes, General, we will keep them at the camp for a few days, long enough for the *inhenicha* to do its work, and then we will ask for the ransom. Yes, General, that is all."

Thomas placed the phone in a waterproof ammo can and turned his attention back to Gwen, staring intently, trying to figure out more about who she was.

In the other dhow, Tanya was also being well treated, even been offered a pint bottle of Guinness stout, which she'd turned down in favor of lukewarm water.

Tanya's rescuers had provided brief introductions, all in English with proper English accents. The leader was named Johnathan; the man at the tiller, Midella; and the other two men were Solomon and Prince Nathan.

"You sound like an American, but you have a Russian name, Miss Tanya," Johnathan announced out of the blue, after minutes of silence.

"It's a Ukrainian name, but my family has been in America for three generations," Tanya replied politely.

"Ah yes, the American cooking pot, with all of the vegetables mixed together for one flavor," Johnathan smiled, showing bright white teeth that contrasted boldly against his very dark skin.

Tanya almost told him to say *melting pot* instead of *cooking pot*, but the description that Johnathan had provided made more sense than her own, so Tanya just smiled and nodded.

"Now we have a long ride. You and your friend will be our guests until your families provide us with a reward for rescuing you." Johnathan grinned.

"You mean a ransom for chasing away our dive boat and kidnapping us," Tanya said with a death stare directed into Johnathan's eyes.

"Such ugly words from such a beautiful lady. Yes, I am sure that your family will pay much for your rescue. They will be very grateful."

"You are criminals! This is against the law, even here," Tanya blurted out, letting her anger get the better of her for a moment.

"Laws of the white man are viewed very differently by many here. Yes, we have the white man's laws written on paper. That paper is in the capital, where all of the white men advise the leaders of the country. We also have laws in our hearts. We did not rape you, and we did not kill you, even though you come to a place where you do not belong to help make more white man's rules. The earth here belongs to us, and what is below the earth belongs to us too, but America, England, and France own the companies that take all of the things under the earth and make themselves richer. You let us hold the papers with your laws now and call us independent, but they are still your laws, not ours. So the laws in our hearts and the laws of our tribes tell us that we can take some things back, inshalla." Johnathan paused, giving Tanya the chance to rebut him.

"So how do you let our families know where we are? They'll think that we drowned and plan our funerals," Tanya said convincingly this time, without the tone of anger she had slipped into before.

"When we get to our village, we will contact the Americans in Lagos and tell them that we need reimbursement for your transportation and rescue. If they agree, we will take you to where we can safely hand you over in return for the money, and you will not see us again."

"And if they refuse to pay?" Tanya asked.

"Then you will be our guests for a long time, but you will be required to work to pay for your food. That is more than fair," Johnathan said a little sternly.

CHAPTER 4

SANTO ANTONIO HARBOR, SÃO TOMÉ
06 1300 JULY

Captain Rodrigues sat impatiently in the office while the São Toméan Coast Guard commander behind the counter—having called the US embassy in Libreville, Gabon—spoke excitedly into the phone, explaining that two Americans had been lost while diving. After a long exchange, the commander hung up the phone and walked around the counter and over to Captain Rodrigues.

Rodrigues stood up as the commander approached; he shifted nervously, never looking the other man in the eye.

"Captain, you stated that the two divers never returned to the surface. Why didn't you remain at anchor and wait for them or go with the current and look for them?" the commander asked skeptically.

"They did not have the air to stay down longer, and I wanted to get back and tell someone so that we could do a proper search before dark. I came straight here, Commander."

"It's a strange coincidence that not more than two hours ago, we heard a call over the radio that was badly broken up, but the caller seemed to say that he was under attack. Did you make that call, Captain?"

"Well, I tried to call, but I was so excited I don't remember what I said. I'll lose my dive boat license," the captain said nervously.

"You will lose your license if you left divers behind, but not if they were stupid and got themselves killed. We need to go to your boat as soon as the police arrive to collect their belongings."

"No need to go to my boat, Commander; I brought their belongings. They're in my car out front."

"How considerate. But I think we will still need to go to your boat. Where is your crewman? Is he still aboard?"

"Of course. He's taking care of the gear."

"Call him right now, and then give me the phone. I want to speak with him," the commander said forcefully.

Captain Rodrigues called the mate on his cell phone and introduced the commander before handing him the phone.

"Who am I speaking with?" the commander demanded.

"This is Michael Santos, the ship's mate," the young man replied.

"Michael, get off the boat *now*. Do not dispose of anything, and do not clean anything. Sit down in the shade and wait for us. Have a beer—or maybe two. The captain and I will be coming to the boat in a few minutes. Do you understand? Tell me what you are going to do, because if you do anything else, you will spend the night in jail."

"I am going to get off the boat, have a beer or two, and wait for you but not take anything off the boat. Can I take two beers? There is no beer on the dock."

"Yes, you can take two beers. We will be there in a few minutes," the commander ended the call and handed the phone back to the captain just as two São Toméan police officers entered the office.

"Thank you for coming so quickly," the commander said to them.

"Have you started the search?" the older of the two police officers asked.

"Yes, I have a boat en route, and a helicopter should be in the air by now and will be in the area in a matter of minutes. Can we all fit into your car and head down to the captain's boat? Captain Rodrigues can tell you what happened on our way there."

Rodrigues went through the story once more, still not mentioning the dhows or the fact that he had left Gwen and Tanya less than an hour into their dive.

When the police car pulled up to the dock where the *Sea Quest* was tied up, Michael was nowhere to be seen.

"Captain, please remain here with this officer while we take a look at your boat. Officer, send someone to pick up Michael Santos. He probably saw the police car and panicked. Why would he panic, Captain?" the commander said with a curious tone.

"Why, I don't know. Maybe he was in some other trouble that I don't know about," Captain Rodrigues said, obviously flustered.

"We won't be long," the commander said as he turned to board the *Sea Quest* with the older police officer.

The commander stepped onto the boat and then turned back around to stare at the captain for a moment. "Are you sure that you don't have anything else to tell me?" he asked the other man patiently.

"Uh, no. I can't think of anything else at the moment," the captain stuttered.

The commander and the police officer methodically searched the boat, starting at the dive platform before moving forward, and then searched the cabin before heading under the pilothouse. The commander found the shotgun on a rack attached to the wall. He pulled the weapon down, checked to see that it was unloaded, and smelled the chamber. He frowned and handed the shotgun to the police officer, who smelled it too before giving the commander a knowing glance.

"This weapon has been fired recently," the police officer said. "I will take it as evidence."

"There are three shells missing from this box of double-ought buckshot. You need to hang onto this too," the commander advised, handing over the box of ammo.

The commander and the police officer emerged from the cabin and jumped off the boat onto the dock. The police officer nodded to his partner to make sure that he had his attention and then stepped forward and placed his hand on his holstered sidearm.

"Captain Rodrigues, you are under arrest for murder. Turn around and place your hands on the side of the car in front of you," the older police officer ordered.

Captain Rodrigues complied, and the younger police officer patted him down and handcuffed him. "It wasn't me! It was the pirates!" Rodrigues yelled out frantically.

"Pirates? So why do you suddenly remember these pirates?" the commander said with a sneer. "Take him away. I will walk back."

CHAPTER 5

ABUJA, NIGERIA
06 2000 JULY

"General O'Finn, the president will see you now," President Mamudu's plump and voluptuous assistant announced officiously.

General O'Finn marched behind the assistant into the president of Nigeria's opulent office. O'Finn moved like a boxer who had been in the ring too many times, bobbing his head awkwardly as he attempted to maintain his old military bearing. The president was on the phone, but he motioned for O'Finn to sit down in an upholstered chair in front of his desk. After almost five minutes of small talk, President Mamudu ended the call.

"Thank you for coming to see me. I have several things that I need to speak with you about. First, you need to keep your pirates on a tighter leash. We both have an interest in keeping outsiders away from our oil operations in Nigeria, but crossing international boundaries and kidnapping Americans is attracting far too much attention. We live in a house of cards, and you are doing things that will bring it all down."

"Mr. President, the explorations in São Tomé experienced several substantial well leaks. If oil had started washing up on the beaches, the São Tomé oil leases would have never been signed," O'Finn explained.

"I understand that, O'Finn, but the *ochistitel* had already been used, and you kidnapped a couple of American scuba divers and then brought them into my country."

"I understand your concerns, and that part was a mistake. The problem is that the *ochistitel* takes two to three weeks to digest the oil and then die from its exposure to saltwater and sunlight. After that, there is no evidence of what could have caused the bleaching on the bottom. The two Americans we kidnapped were scientists working on a UN grant, collecting samples in an active area. There is a good chance that they may have figured out what we are doing."

"Yes, yes, but not again, do you understand? The international damage from this episode was significant."

"Yes, sir, I understand. But remember, it is better to have the oil fall to the bottom and destroy the reefs that nobody can see than it is to have the oil wash into the mangroves and affect the shrimp-fishery industry. That would have a significant economic impact, Mr. President."

"Yes, yes, I understand all that, which is why I tolerate your presence and pay you exorbitant sums of money to take care of this problem. Now, I have two other concerns that we need to discuss. You have already expressed to me the importance of keeping the *ochistitel* secret, but triple S has informed me that copious amounts of the shipments from Russia are being diverted. If the *ochistitel* ends up in Cameroon or even the United Kingdom and their scientists figure out how it works, there will be an outcry to stop making it, and the Russians will bow to that pressure. Along those same lines, triple S is concerned that the Russian employees of your company are involved in many things outside the scope of your contract—weapons and drug smuggling and even espionage."

"Mr. President, you know that the oil business is a tough one, and boys will be boys. When we find them behaving badly and affecting our operations, we send them back. There are always new ones willing to work."

"And the espionage?"

"That's the way of the world, Mr. President. You know that some of these guys will go back and report to their government. If triple S finds something specific, by all means, arrest them, but this is probably just a lot of speculation. You know how those intelligence people can be."

"Yes, I do. And now I have American intelligence breathing down my neck and sending more people into my country to look for the hostages due to your stupidity. Now, good day, General O'Finn," the president said as he picked up the phone and rang his assistant. "Savia, please escort General O'Finn out of the building. He has no other business here today."

CHAPTER 6

FAUQUIER COUNTY, VA
07 0700 JULY

Jim Stillwater had just settled into his high-backed leather office chair and was watching a pileated woodpecker knock away at a dead branch on an oak tree not far from his second-story home-office window. CNN was on the big-screen TV with the sound muted, and the Reuters news feed was sharing space with Jim's e-mail on his computer screen. The woodpecker finally flew away to another tree, so Jim turned back to his computer and continued to go through his e-mail, occasionally glancing up at what was showing on CNN. He saw a story about Russian organized crime and their fondness for using auto racing to launder money, and he grabbed the clicker to turn on the sound.

As Ralph Splitter, the bearded reporter, was talking dramatically while race cars continued to roar around the track in the background, Jim's phone rang. He muted the TV again before putting down the clicker and picking up the phone. "Hello, this is Jim," he answered.

"This is Ian Lovelost from the US State Department. Is this Mr. Jim Stillwater?"

"Yes, that's me," Jim said, while checking his caller ID.

"Mr. Stillwater, you are listed as the emergency contact on Gwen Stillwater's passport, and I am most saddened to inform you that Gwen Stillwater is missing at sea and presumed dead."

"Missing at sea? She was doing a scientific survey on the coral reef in less than thirty feet of water. There must be some kind of mistake," Jim answered, his voice rising at the end.

"Mr. Stillwater, the São Toméan police have arrested one suspect and are seeking one other in what they believe to be a possible homicide," the officer said in a very businesslike tone. "There is an air and sea search underway. Neither Gwen Stillwater nor her diving companion has been found yet."

"Is there someone in São Tomé I can speak to?" Jim asked.

"Mr. Stillwater, I am afraid that due to cutbacks, we do not have an embassy in São Tomé, and the ambassador to São Tomé resides at the US Embassy in Libreville, Gabon. Ambassador Christine Lofftree has asked me to express her condolences and has offered to assist you with transferring Gwen Stillwater's remains should they be found."

"OK, give me the ambassador's number," Jim ordered.

"Yes, of course. But please realize that the phone service is not particularly reliable in that part of the world," Ian advised.

"I once spent a good deal of time in that part of the world. I will be heading to São Tomé on the first flight I can get," Jim added.

"Very well. If you are ready to copy, I will give you my number and the ambassador's number now."

"Yeah, go ahead," Jim replied. He copied both numbers down, read them back, and abruptly ended the call. He then punched in the ambassador's number and, on the third try, reached her secretary. The secretary was expecting Jim's call and put him through to the ambassador without delay.

"Mr. Stillwater, this is Ambassador Lofftree. I am so sorry for your loss. What can I do to help?"

"First of all, it is my understanding that there is a search underway. Is that correct?"

"There is a search underway, but the captain of the dive boat has already been arrested for murder. They found a shotgun on his boat that had been fired, and he has lied repeatedly to the investigator. The ship's mate is also a suspect but is not yet in custody."

"What was the motive?" Jim asked impatiently.

"They haven't provided those details yet. I will be traveling to São Tomé tomorrow, and I promise that I will pass along any additional details that the authorities provide me. Is this the best number to reach you at?"

"Actually, I'll be heading to São Tomé on the first flight I can get, so please use my cell number," Jim returned in a calmer tone.

"I have that; Ian already passed it along. Please understand that there are not many flights into São Tomé. You can connect through Lisbon, Portugal, or Lagos, Nigeria. There are direct flights from here, in Libreville, but getting to Libreville is almost as difficult as getting to São Tomé."

"I don't plan to ever go back to Lagos, so hopefully I can get a flight through Lisbon," Jim said.

"I'm glad you have been to Africa before. That's good—you know what to expect. This will be nothing like dealing with authorities in the United States," the ambassador said, a slight warning in her tone.

"Ambassador, thank you very much," Jim said sincerely.

"Mr. Stillwater, please call Ian with your travel arrangements so that he can make sure that we get together in São Tomé when you arrive."

As soon as his conversation with the ambassador ended, Jim called his corporate travel agent and made arrangements to arrive in São Tomé via Lisbon on Tuesday afternoon. His next call was to his boss. "Joe, I am going to need to take some time off, like you suggested," Jim started off.

"That's great! Good decision, Jim," Joe said in a genuinely happy tone.

"This won't be a vacation, Joe. I was contacted by the US State Department this morning as there is an ongoing air and sea search for Gwen and Tanya. The authorities have also arrested the dive boat captain on suspicion of murder," Jim said, struggling to get the words out.

"Jim, take whatever time you need. You're going to São Tomé, I expect?"

"I arrive Tuesday afternoon. The ambassador lives in Gabon but will be flying in on Monday, so I will have some support from State while I'm there."

"I'm going to call Morgan and send her along. You should not be taking care of this on your own."

"I won't turn that down, Joe."

"And I'll be over this afternoon, if you want."

"No need. I'll be busy doing research for the trip."

"I'll bring my laptop and help you out. I know you can use the company with both kids out of the house now," Joe offered.

"OK, sounds good."

"Hang in there, Jim. I'll call Morgan and head over as soon as I can."

"Thanks, Joe. See you soon," Jim said, ending the call.

Jim went back online and began to immerse himself in anything and everything that had even a remote connection to São Tomé and the Gulf of Guinea. Two hours had gone by before he knew it. A sudden loud warning bark from his playful but protective German shepherd Mosby prompted Jim to instinctively click the bottom of his computer screen and bring up his driveway camera feed. Jim smiled when he saw both Joe and Morgan walking toward the house with armloads of bags and a couple of six-packs of beer.

Jim yelled out to Mosby to go to his waiting place and opened the door just as Joe and Morgan were coming up the steps. Morgan set bags of food and one six-pack down on the steps before jumping forward to give Jim a hug. Joe tucked a bag of sandwiches under his left arm, held the other six-pack, and gave Jim a one-armed *bro hug*.

"Wow, I didn't expect to see both of you or all of this food. Come on in. You can set it all on the kitchen table," Jim said as he ushered his friends into the house. Mosby could stand this intrusion no longer; the dog ran into the great room and bounced between the two guests, licking their hands and finally sitting in front of Morgan, expecting the routine scratches from her long nails.

"Jim, is there any news?" Morgan asked before Joe could.

"No, but I know how well both Tanya and Gwen can take care of themselves in the water, and I can't help but believe that I'll get a ransom request from pirates—that or the São Toméan Coast Guard will find them floating around near the dive site."

Joe and Morgan nodded in agreement.

"I'll be right back, Jim. I need to get our laptops out of the trunk," Joe said as he headed out the door.

"Jim, I called Hans, and he'll be coming tomorrow to house-sit and keep an eye on Mosby for you. I think retirement is boring the hell out of him. He wanted it to be a surprise, but I thought that you might need some help getting one of the spare rooms ready—" Morgan awkwardly cut herself off before she finished with *since Gwen isn't here.*

"Thanks, Morgan. It'll be good to see Colonel Becker. It's going to be tough waiting around here to get started on the trip. But there just aren't that many flights into São Tomé, and it's better to wait here than take a two-day layover in Lisbon."

"What time is your flight tomorrow?" Joe asked as he came back through the front door with a laptop bag in each hand.

"I fly out of Dulles on United tomorrow night at ten twenty and arrive in Lisbon Monday morning around ten. Then I'll be stuck in Lisbon for a day since the flights to São Tomé run on only Tuesdays and Thursdays on TAP Air," Jim said with a slight frown.

"At least you'll have some time to recover from the jet lag in Lisbon and will be in better shape when you arrive in São Tomé," Joe said in an encouraging tone.

"Jim, we didn't think you would take the time to go out and grab food, so we stopped by the Orlean Market on the way here and picked up some sandwiches and beer. The pulled pork is still hot, so dig in, OK?" Morgan offered as she finished scratching Mosby.

"You guessed right; I am starved, and these smell really good," Jim said as he reached in to one of the bags and fished out a large pulled-pork sandwich and one of the containers of coleslaw. Mosby crawled under the table, anxiously waiting for someone to accidentally drop a tasty morsel.

Morgan was already retrieving silverware from the kitchen drawer and a church key for the beer.

"I see you picked up some of the local brews," Jim said as he popped open a Devil's Backbone Vienna Lager. "I also have the normal selection in the beer fridge if you want one of those."

Joe and Morgan pulled sandwiches and food containers out of the bags and spread them across the table, while Jim grabbed plates and began to devour his pulled pork.

"Jim, who knew that Gwen and Tanya were going to São Tomé?" Morgan asked.

"Just about anybody who might be interested. It was a UN grant, and Tanya gained approval for her participation through the park service. Gwen and Tanya have been in touch with I don't know how many scientists around the world who have done field work in São Tomé. So, there's no easy way to narrow that down. I'm focusing on motive. There was no robbery—none of her things are missing. She didn't have any enemies in São Tomé, and there aren't any terrorists there that I'm aware of. That's why I keep thinking pirates. They were less than three hundred miles from the Niger Delta, and the pirates there have gone out for more than four hundred miles in the past."

"Yeah, they were doing that off Somalia too. It blows my mind how far they go in those little boats to get out to the shipping lanes," Joe added.

"Hey, Jim, can you give me a copy of your itinerary? I'm going to try and mirror your flights. Joe did tell you that I was going along," Morgan said with a raised eyebrow.

Jim hurried back upstairs to his office and returned with an armload of assorted papers. He took the stack over to the bar between the kitchen and dining room and pulled his itinerary out of the tangle of maps and travel brochures that Gwen had collected prior to her trip. "Here you go. I think the United flight is booked, but there is a Lufthansa flight that leaves around the same time," Jim offered as he handed Morgan his itinerary.

Morgan pulled out her cell phone and walked into the library, reading the itinerary before calling the travel agency. Jim and Joe continued to eat their meals and had popped open their second beers before Morgan returned.

"Yep, you were right, Jim. United was booked, so I'm on a Lufthansa flight about an hour ahead of yours—and I'm paying about a hundred bucks more—but I got onto the same flight into São Tomé on Tuesday," Morgan announced as she came back into the room and started to fill her plate with food.

"Jim, I would come too, and if you decide that you need me over there, I'll take the Thursday flight into São Tomé. In the meantime, I'll be working the good ol' boy networks hard throughout the community to see if I can dig anything up that will help," Joe said, suddenly very serious.

"That's a good plan, Joe. None of us have a network half as broad as yours, so if you can't dig something up, nobody can," Jim said as Morgan nodded in agreement.

"Yes, and I'll be performing Jim Stillwater control and hopefully charming information out of the São Toméan authorities instead of beating it out of them," Morgan teased.

Jim and Joe both smiled as they devoured more of the fresh deli food.

A second later, the landline rang, and Jim jumped up to answer it, hoping for news of Gwen. "Hello, this is Jim," he answered with anticipation in his voice.

"Mr. Stillwater, how are you doing? Is there any good news yet?" Colonel Hans Becker asked.

"Nothing yet, Hans. Thanks for coming down to hold the fort."

"No problem at all, but there has been a slight change in plans. Jorge is flying in with his boys to hold down the fort and take care of Mosby. I am leaving tonight and arriving in São Tomé via Lagos, so I might even beat you there, Mr. Stillwater."

"Dude, you did not need to do that," Jim said, somewhat shocked.

"Well, you know I have some friends at the consulate in Lagos, and one of the guys I served with in Iraq is now chief of security for Fossil Petroleum. I might have mentioned his name before—Griz Grizwalski?" Hans asked and paused.

"Actually, I remember him. We met up in New York at that German bar. Big athletic bald guy with a great sense of humor."

"Yeah, tough as nails too. So he might be able to come through with some different connections than we have."

"That would be helpful. So when does Jorge get in?" Jim asked.

"He and his sons Miles and Patrick are coming out via the red-eye, so I wouldn't be surprised if they got there early tomorrow morning," Hans replied.

"Jorge and Mosby sure do get along, so that's gonna work out great. You guys are incredible," Jim said as he shook his head in disbelief over how fast his friends had readjusted their lives to help him out.

"Jim, let me talk to Morgan for a minute, if you don't mind."

"He wants to talk to you," Jim said as he handed the phone to Morgan.

"So how is he doing?" Hans inquired quietly.

"Good. He's optimistic and has a lot of faith in Gwen and Tanya to get themselves out of trouble. He's convinced that it's pirates," Morgan added.

"He might be right. I hope so. I just don't want you to be on Jim Stillwater control by yourself if someone hurts Gwen," Hans said seriously, even quieter.

"Yeah, I get that. I'm glad you're coming, Hans. We will see you on Tuesday."

"OK, see you then." Hans ended the call.

CHAPTER 7

NIGER DELTA, NIGERIA
08 1000 JULY

Gwen and Tanya sat facing each other on plastic lawn furniture inside a shack made of sheets of corrugated steel and wooden pallets. The floor was hard-packed dirt, and the place smelled like urine and old garbage cans.

"At least they didn't tie us up," Gwen said to Tanya, who looked back and frowned.

"I don't think they're all that worried about two blond white women sneaking away unnoticed. As Johnathan said, if others take us hostage, they might not treat us as nicely," Tanya said as she peered through a crack in the metal wall.

"They had an entire floating oil rig pulled up into the mangroves. I wonder what else they're up to. There's even an old Victorian house on the hill at the edge of the camp," Gwen said with astonishment.

"Yeah, I was watching a bunch of the pirates when we came into the harbor, and it looks like they've been practicing climbing up that oil rig. I guess they're going to hijack one of those next," Tanya said, smiling in grudging admiration at their seemingly outrageous goal.

"How long do you think we'll be stuck here? We don't have anti-malaria drugs, and the mosquitoes are eating us alive," Gwen said as she swatted a mosquito on her neck.

"Hopefully days and not weeks, but if they ransom us, there will be negotiations, proof of life, and then the exchange. That will take at least a week, and it might take a month or more," Tanya said as she seemed to calculate the timeline as she spoke.

"The longer it takes, the more likely a rescue too," Gwen added.

"Have you seen how many armed men they have? They're basically one of those underground armies in a bad spy movie," Tanya said.

"There is something strange about this whole thing. These guys are far too disciplined for a run-of-the-mill pirate group—or even a guerrilla army. Even big groups like Boko Haram operate more like armed street gangs then military units, especially in their base camps."

"I've noticed the military discipline too. Someone is training them," Tanya added.

Their conversation was interrupted by a bang on the open shack door. A slender African woman in her thirties entered the shack. "Gwen, Tanya, my name is Mila. It is your turn to go to the dining facility. Please come with me," she said as she turned around and walked back through the door.

Gwen and Tanya exchanged baffled glances but jumped to their feet and followed Mila. The woman led them along a row of more than twenty shacks to a long corrugated-metal structure that looked surprisingly modern and new among the ramshackle shacks. "It is the women's turn to eat now," Mila explained as she led them into the large building that was apparently the dining hall.

"So, are they all hostages too?" Gwen asked, gesturing to the other women in the room.

"No, just you two and an Australian couple and their sailboat. The rest of us are wives, girlfriends, or former hostages from other tribes who decided to stay. The food is good; you will see," Mila said as she grabbed metal-rimmed plates from a stack near the door and handed one to Gwen and one to Tanya.

Gwen smelled food cooking and suddenly realized how hungry she was. Mila led the way to the counter and handed her plate to a woman behind the counter, who was stirring a big steaming pot on a propane burner. The woman scooped a generous ladle of fish stew and a dollop of cassava from another pot onto the plate and handed it back to Mila. The process was repeated for Gwen and Tanya, although their portions seemed a little bit smaller than the ones provided to Mila.

"We keep our own forks and spoons, but you can grab some plastic ones out of the box by the window," Mila said, pointing as she sat down at an unoccupied table in the middle of the room. There were at least thirty women, all African, sitting at the other tables in small groups; they matched in their colorful traditional attire and the darkness of their skin.

Mila was already almost finished with her fish stew when Gwen and Tanya rejoined her at the table and opened the little plastic packages containing a spork and a napkin that had yellow markings strikingly similar to those of an American fast-food burger outlet.

Gwen got the plastic wrapper off her utensil first and dug into the fish stew, mixing it with a bit of the cassava. The food was good, and Gwen looked up at Tanya, who gave her an approving nod as she placed another forkful of fish into her mouth. She washed it down with water from one of about nine water bottles that were grouped in the middle of the table. *This is a good sign*, Gwen thought, having feared that they would be forced to drink dirty water from a local source and suffer the inevitable results.

"How long has this place been here?" Tanya asked Mila, who was eating silently.

"I have been here for almost two years," Mila replied between mouthfuls.

"So, ah, how does it remain like this for so long?" Tanya asked, clearly puzzled.

"You mean why has the army not come here to rescue you? Do not get your hopes up about that. There is some kind of agreement that I am not important enough to know everything about. I do know that the Nigerian army is run by Muslim generals who fought against these tribes in the Biafran war. You Americans have such a short memory. You once helped Biafra, but now you help Nigeria, since they have the oil and Western oil companies want to get rich with it. What is important for you to know is that nobody from the government will come here to rescue you. When your family brings the money for your return, we will give you back, with a promise from you that you will never come back here. If we catch you twice, you will be killed. If you try to escape, we will catch you twice, and you will be killed. Now, eat your food, and we will get you back to your temporary home."

"Can we go outside our shack?" Gwen asked.

"Of course. You can go to the outhouse, and you can come here. When you get back, there will be two cots, mosquito net, and a lantern in your house. If you go anywhere else, we will assume that you have decide to escape, and you will be shot, even if your family has agreed to pay to get you back. Do you both understand that?" Gwen and Tanya nodded. "And do white girls have brains that rattle when they nod, or will you use your tongues?" Mila asked in a suddenly harsh tone.

"Yes, I understand," Gwen answered and looked to Tanya.

"Yes, I understand too," Tanya replied.

"All right. Good. When you are finished with your food, I will take you back so there is no mistake about which way to go. Since they took away your watches, I will come get you at mealtimes, as we eat after the soldiers. Don't worry, ladies, you will not be here long."

Tanya glanced over to a nearby table and noticed four women playing a game that involved moving some sort of round tokens into wooden bowls on a small game board. "What are they playing?" she asked Mila, remembering her hostage-survival training.

"That is mancala, but you will not be here long enough to learn how to play. Hopefully," Mila added after a pause. "All right, let's get you back so you can get settled. Keep your plastic and put your plates over there. The ladies will wash the plates and sanitize them so nobody gets dysentery," Mila explained as she got up and deposited her empty plate in a bin on a table by one of the exit doors.

Gwen and Tanya followed Mila through the back door of the dining facility on the opposite side of the building from where they had come in. As they stepped back out into the harsh sunshine, Tanya looked up the hill behind the building and noticed a fenced compound with a sentry at the gate. Inside the fenced area were hundreds of fifty-gallon oil drums stacked three high on pallets. Tanya immediately started thinking about how she could ignite the collection of what she believed must be smuggled oil or gasoline into a distracting conflagration.

Gwen saw where Tanya was staring and decided to explore the issue. "Mila, what are all of those drums for—are your soldiers stockpiling oil?" Gwen asked.

"It is not oil. It is none of your business, is what it is. Just stay away from there. You understand?" Mila said harshly.

Gwen nodded and walked around the corner of the building with Mila and Tanya, putting the compound out of sight. A booming voice from behind them made them all stop in their tracks and turn. "Mila, my lady, I see that you are taking good care of our guests," Johnathan said as he jogged up behind the women from the other side of the building.

"Johnathan, you startled me. Yes, I have explained the rules, and they have had lunch."

"Miss Tanya and Just Gwen, did you get enough to eat?" Johnathan asked.

Gwen and Tanya nodded, which brought a stern look to Mila's face for a moment. "The food was good," Tanya retorted. "But what does that matter if you're going to kill us?"

"Kill—you? Oh no. You are much too valuable. I have already sent a message to the consulate in Lagos saying that you are safe after being rescued at sea, and it only cost us four hundred thousand US dollars in time and fuel to rescue you. So next, they will want a picture. Let me show you my new phone. I can make a movie and send it to them. Mila, stand between them while I start."

"What the fuck?" Gwen blurted out.

"Please humor me. Stand with Mila, and I will ask whether you are being treated well. You answer yes, and your families will pay the price to see you again. OK?"

"Gwen, just do this," Tanya urged.

Gwen and Tanya stood on either side of Mila, and Johnathan turned his camera on in movie mode.

"Gwen and Tanya, your captain left you in the ocean, and we rescued you. Now, after a reward is paid for our services, you will be returned to your families. Are you being treated well? Are you OK?"

Gwen and Tanya nodded in agreement, and Gwen made an obscene gesture with her left hand and held it beside her leg while she smiled.

"Thank you, ladies. I will send this along to Lagos, and hopefully we can speed you back to your families. Mila, show them back to their place and go find one of your girlfriends to join us. I am finished working for the day and need some relaxation," Johnathan ordered as he turned and departed in the opposite direction.

Mila led Gwen and Tanya back to their shack. In addition to the cots with mosquito netting that had been promised, there were a case of bottled water, two washbasins, and a jerry can of water labeled "NO DRINK."

"I am sorry that I cannot provide you with other clothing," Mila said, pointing at the stinger suits that Gwen and Tanya were still wearing over their bikinis. "You can use the water in the can to wash your clothes. Just don't use it to wash your faces," she warned.

"Thank you, Mila," Tanya said in an overly charming tone that surprised Gwen and prompted a bemused look.

"Yes, thank you," Gwen said hesitantly, following Tanya's lead.

Mila turned and headed through the door but paused for a moment at the threshold. "I will send some pallets later so you won't need to wash on the mud floor," she said as she walked out of the shack.

CHAPTER 8

LAGOS, NIGERIA
09 1800 JULY

The Lufthansa Airbus taxied to the terminal at Lagos International Airport. Hans looked out the window and saw a mobile stairway being rolled up to the side of the plane. Minutes later, a very German-looking fortysomething flight attendant, who seemed to be in charge, pushed open the door of the airplane, and the hot, humid West African air poured inside. Hans easily grabbed his carry-on bag from the overhead bin. He was more than six feet tall, and in spite of middle age, still slender enough to move easily in the narrow aisle. Dodging two other passengers who seemed to be in a panicked hurry, Hans stepped into the aisle of the otherwise half-empty plane, and jostled his way forward past two rows to the open door and into the bright afternoon sun.

Hans thanked the flight attendant as he stepped through the doorway and felt the mobile stairs wobble enough to make him uncomfortable. He headed straight for the luggage carousel inside the terminal. After a twenty-minute wait inside the barely air-conditioned entry hall, he saw his bag, grabbed it, and headed for the immigration and customs checkpoints. The immigration officer barely looked at his passport before waving him forward, but the customs officer at the next station seemed to be irritated by Hans's presence.

"What is the nature of your business in Lagos?" he demanded officiously as he held out Hans's passport and examined it from several different angles.

"I am en route to São Tomé and am just spending the night here while I wait for my flight," Hans replied tiredly.

"Your flight to São Tomé leaves tomorrow?" the customs officer prompted suspiciously as he paged through Hans's passport.

"Yes, just one night here," Hans repeated.

"Please open your bags and place the contents on the table," the customs officer said in what was suddenly a bored tone of voice.

Hans frowned but began to comply. He was scooping out a layer of clothing from his larger suitcase, trying to keep the items folded as he placed them on the table, and was startled when he heard the booming voice of Griz Grizwalski behind the customs officer on the other side of the checkpoint.

"Soloman, why are you fucking with my friend Hans?"

The customs officer was startled too and turned to find Griz standing uncomfortably close to him. "Mr. Grizwalski, is this man a friend of yours?" he asked in a slightly amused tone.

"Damn right he is, Soloman. This man is a steely-eyed killer whom I had the pleasure to serve with in combat."

"He is a killer?" Soloman asked, alarmed.

"He only kills the bad guys and the occasional person who really pisses him off, so I hope that the two of you are getting along OK," Griz said with a deadpan voice as Hans rolled his eyes.

"Mr. Grizwalski, he was just telling me about his trip to São Tomé tomorrow. We were having a wonderful conversation," Soloman said while nodding and looking to Hans for confirmation.

"Yes, we were having a very pleasant conversation," Hans said, playing along. He started to put his things back into his bag as Soloman offered him a relieved smile and handed him his passport, boarding passes, and itinerary.

"I am glad to hear that, Soloman. Hans, great to see you. I have a car waiting for us outside. After I heard you were flying in, I made some plans for this evening. Glad I got here before you took a taxi too. You might have ended up in a ditch without your shit. Ain't that right, Soloman?" Griz said as he turned to face the customs officer.

"Yes, Mr. Grizwalski, Lagos can be a dangerous place, so I am so glad that you came here to take care of your friend."

Griz handed Soloman an envelope and motioned for Hans to follow him.

Hans hurriedly rezipped his bag, gave a smile and a wave to Soloman, and turned to follow Griz past a police checkpoint on the other side of customs. Griz pushed through the crowd, leading the way to a white Chevy Suburban waiting at the curb just outside the airport's exit. Two large and incredibly fit Caucasians waited at the front and back of the vehicle and opened the rear doors for Griz and Hans to get in. Once they were inside the vehicle, the two body-guards jumped into the front seats and slammed the heavy armored doors.

Griz seemed to relax and smiled at Hans, holding out his hand to shake. "It's good to see you, brother. You picked one hell of a place for a one-night layover," Griz teased.

"It was either here or someplace where I didn't know anyone in town," Hans said with a smile.

"You need to make more friends in the friendly parts of the world." Griz chuckled.

"Actually, I needed to make last-minute arrangements, and this was the fastest way to get to São Tomé. My best friend's wife is missing in São Tomé. They have her officially listed as missing, but her husband seems to think that we might be getting a ransom demand soon," Hans said with a serious look as the Suburban weaved through several airport checkpoints far too fast. Soon, another white Suburban started following them.

"Ah shit. I am so sorry to hear about that, Hans. When did she go missing?" Griz asked in a suddenly businesslike tone.

"Friday. She was diving with another American woman who is also a friend of mine," Hans answered.

"Diving? Might have been sharks. Might have been an accident," Griz said introspectively. "Why in hell did they come all the way to São Tomé just to go diving?"

"They were on a UN-funded grant to survey the reef. One is a marine biologist and the other is a naturalist for the US Park Service," Hans replied.

Griz's whole demeanor suddenly changed. Shifting his focus from the road ahead, he turned and looked straight into Hans's eyes as he talked. "I think your best friend is right; he will probably get a ransom demand in the next few days. There's a lot of weird shit goin' on here. And your friends sure fit the profile. Good news is, for a few hundred thousand dollars, they will likely be returned safe and sound in another couple of weeks."

"That is good news, if you're right," Hans said skeptically. "But what's really going on?"

"Back in the sixties, Nigeria was the front line of the Muslim versus Christian—or, more accurately, Muslim versus non-Muslim—struggle that we see in so many places around the world today. Their civil war pitted the non-Muslim tribes in the southeast, the Igbos, against the Huasa and Fulanis in the northeast and the Yorubas in the west. Biafra, the region in the southeast, was home to the Igbos, and although almost nobody calls that area 'Biafra' anymore, it is still largely non-Muslim and also the poorest part of the country, despite its being the source of most of Nigeria's oil. Piracy and gasoline smuggling are now the biggest sources of income in that region."

"I remember hearing about the Biafran war, with all of the starving children." Hans nodded.

"Yeah, the United States was officially neutral in the civil war, but after the Yorubas tried to starve Biafra into submission and all of those pictures of starving kids hit the media, the United States provided food aid. A lot of Yorubas blame us for lengthening the civil war because of that food aid," Griz said as he looked out the window.

"Incredible," Hans replied, shaking his head. "But I thought that the piracy got cleaned up a few years back."

"It did. The Nigerian government hired a retired US general by the name of O'Finn, and he clamped down hard with a large group of mercenaries who are officially oil company security guards. O'Finn is the CEO of an engineering services company that also provides security, logistics, and anything else that will make him a buck in parts of the world most legit engineering companies consider too high risk to bother with. He got his foot in the door in Nigeria with a contract for oil-spill mitigation. He uses some sort of proprietary Russian technology that I don't fully understand for cleanups. Provides his own security for the oil-spill cleanup operations too. When he started out, he was hiring mainly former British SAS guys and former French Foreign Legion. Recently, we started seeing a lot of Russians. Their tattoos and a few other tells give away that they are former Spetsnaz. A couple of my staff think that they may not actually be former, but that seems a little bit paranoid to me."

"That model has been used before. During the Angolan civil war, the oil company that had the lease in the Cabinda enclave formed the largest private army in the world to keep both sides at bay. The Spetsnaz operated that way in the Ukraine, so maybe your staff are on to something."

"The oil must flow," Griz said with a grin.

"So, let me guess: the merc army that was formed to get rid of the pirates decided that they were not getting paid enough, or some of them went native."

"That's what I thought until recently. One thing doesn't fit though. These pirates never attack any of the oil company people or the oil field infrastructure. They do however kidnap anyone else who shows up in the area."

"That's kinda smart. Especially if the mercs are doing some of the kidnapping to supplement their income," Hans mused.

"And O'Finn seems to still be running the show. He spends about a week out of every month over here and usually pays a visit to the president while he's in town."

"The president of your company?" Hans asked.

"Yeah, him too, but I meant the president of Nigeria," Griz said as he held his company badge up to the guard at the gate outside the hotel. "OK, Hans. We're here."

The big Suburbans weaved through a chicane, past another set of guards who seemed more military from their appearance, and pulled up to the front door of the hotel. Attentive doormen rushed to the car, but before they could get to the doors of the Suburban, two bodyguards from the trailing vehicle opened the doors and shielded Hans and Griz as they exited.

"Welcome to the Lagos Hunton, gentlemen. May I carry any bags for you?" the head doorman asked politely.

"No, thank you. My men will take care of them, but thank you for your attention," Griz said as he handed the doorman a small wad of naira. "He is the only one checking in," Griz added, pointing at Hans.

"Do you have time for a drink at the bar after I get checked in?" Hans asked Griz.

"Damn right I do. I would have been a bit pissed off if you had headed straight to your room for a nap," Griz said with a smile, only half joking.

Hans checked into the hotel uneventfully. He dropped his suit-case and backpack off in the room with the help of one of Griz's bodyguards and headed down to the bar. Griz had already ordered a couple of beers and was looking over the food menu when Hans arrived.

"What took you so long? I'm already on my second beer!" Griz joked.

"I was having sex with the maid," Hans joked back as he grabbed the pint glass in front of the empty seat that Griz gestured to. "Cheers," he said as he raised his glass to toast his friend.

"Cheers. It's good to see you, old buddy," Griz said, raising his own glass. "Now, tell me, why the hell are you goin' to São Tomé? Under these circumstances, there is nothing there but trouble for you."

"Just trying to help a friend and maybe keep him out of trouble if he gets too aggressive trying to find out what happened to his wife," Hans said between sips of beer.

"I get it, Hans. We gotta stick by our friends. So where's your friend now?"

"I would guess that Jim is in Lisbon. He's scheduled to change planes there. Not a whole lotta choices when you're headed to São Tomé."

"Too bad we aren't doing any ferry runs in the company chopper over that way. I could have probably worked something out. The one thing I can do is check in with a few friends at the embassy to see if I can find anything out. If you join me for dinner, we'll probably bump into someone who can help us out. There just aren't that many safe places to eat around here," Griz said.

"That sounds good, Griz. I should be able to get a nap in before then so I don't fall asleep in my soup."

"Well, a couple beers should help with that," Griz said as he motioned to the waiter for another round.

Two very attractive tall North African women walked up to the table. "Do you mind if we sit down? You two look like you could use some company," one of them offered.

"Piss off," Griz said without even looking up at them. The women paused, waiting for a response from Hans.

"I said get the fuck away, before I call hotel security," Griz said, glancing up briefly before he turned back to Hans, the women walking away. "The hookers get pretty thick in here. They are beautiful and talented, but most have HIV."

"So that's still a big problem here?"

"I assume you mean the HIV, so yes, but prostitution is run by organized crime here, and most of the girls are brought in from elsewhere, so they're far from any family who would help them if they decided to quit the business."

"Same story in Europe," Hans replied before taking another sip of his drink.

Hans and Griz caught each other up on old friends, and after his third beer, Hans headed up to his room. He looked at his watch and noted that Griz would be back to pick him up for dinner in less than four hours. Back in his room, he set up a wake-up call, put the desk chair in front of the door, and turned the lock. Hans tried to call Jim but got a message saying that the number was not currently in service, so he decided that Jim must have still been on a plane. He then pulled a change of clothes for dinner out of his now badly packed suitcase and finally showered before hitting the sack. His head had barely hit the pillow before he was asleep.

It seemed like less than five minutes had gone by when the phone next to the bed rang and jolted Hans from a sound sleep. He looked at the clock before he picked up the phone, surprised that two hours had passed.

"Sir, this is your wake-up call," a polite female voice announced.

"Thank you," Hans said before hanging up the phone. It took him several attempts to properly fit the handset into the cradle.

Hans checked his cell phone and noticed that he had text messages from both Jim and Morgan, confirming that they had arrived safely in Lisbon. He dialed Jim, and on the fourth ring, a groggy-sounding Jim Stillwater answered.

"Hello, ah, hello, this is Jim."

"Mr. Stillwater, you sound like you just woke up from a nap!" Hans teased.

"Yeah, you got that right. Morgan and I linked up at the airport and had lunch in town and a drink at the hotel before we decided to fend off the jet lag with siestas."

"That sounds like my day, only you had better-looking company than I had."

"So you linked up with your friend OK?" Jim asked.

"Yes, in fact, I did. I also just woke up from a nap, and Griz is picking me up for dinner in less than an hour. If you are right about the pirates, Griz is going to be a big help."

"Yeah, I thought he might be," Jim said, sounding more coherent as he woke up.

"So, I take it there is no news yet?"

"No. Morgan and I called Ambassador Lofftree. She's already in São Tomé and is staying in the hotel we are booked at. No news, but the search is still underway."

"OK, Jim. I'll let you go back to sleep, and I'll see you in São Tomé tomorrow. Anything else I can do?"

"No, Hans, you're doing enough already. Have fun with your buddy, and I'll see you tomorrow," Jim said.

"OK. Out here, Mr. Stillwater," Hans said as he hung up.

After taking another shower to wake himself up and getting dressed in suitcase-wrinkled clothes, he headed down to the hotel lobby to meet Griz for dinner and what he expected would be a long night of drinking and storytelling.

CHAPTER 9

SÃO TOMÉ INTERNATIONAL AIRPORT, SÃO TOMÉ
10 1630 JULY

Jim woke up when the flight attendant was moving through the cabin to check seat belts.

"Sir, we will be landing soon. Can I check your seat belt?" the pleasant flight attendant asked.

Jim frowned at what sounded like a stupid reason to wake him up but soon realized that the blanket on his lap was covering the seat belt and pulled it aside to show that his seat belt was buckled.

"Thank you, sir," the flight attendant said before she moved on.

"Wow, you were really out," Morgan said in a surprised tone, a concerned look on her face.

"Yeah, it's getting harder to ignore jet lag as I get older. When I was in my thirties, I thought jet lag was some imaginary excuse that lazy people used to sleep more. I get it now."

"I notice it, but it isn't a big problem. Unfortunately, I can't sleep soundly on airplanes like you can."

"I learned to do that when I was packed into an airplane with a parachute, a reserve chute, and a rucksack. The engine noise seems to help too. I mentioned that I always fell asleep on airplanes to my flight instructor when we were talking about traveling to Europe. It cracked me up when she got a truly horrified look on her face that didn't go away until I mentioned that I meant when I was a passenger, not when I was flying."

Morgan laughed. "Oh, that is funny. I'll bet she kept a close eye on you from the right seat during that flight."

The airliner started to bank to the left, and Jim looked out over the waters surrounding São Tomé, staring intently now at the emerald-green-and-cerulean-blue seascape on the freak chance that he would see some sign of Gwen. Morgan realized what he was doing and started to say something to comfort him but thought better of it. The pilot leveled the wings, and Jim heard the landing gear being lowered into position. The nose of the airplane pitched up, and they all felt a gentle bump as the airplane touched down and then braked hard on the relatively short runway.

Jim and Morgan were off the airplane in a few minutes. They cleared customs and immigration without any issues and headed straight to the rental-car counter to pick up a car. Jim considered waiting for Hans, but his need to find out any news about Gwen won out, so he headed to the hotel where he knew the ambassador was also staying.

"Hans is getting his own car, so he can meet us at the hotel," Jim said somewhat apologetically to Morgan.

"I understand, and Hans wouldn't expect you to wait for him under these circumstances, Jim."

Jim gave Morgan an appreciative nod and headed toward the rental parking lot like a man on a mission. He found the car in the small lot, and the two of them loaded their bags into the tiny bright-yellow Suzuki Vitara. Without delay, they got in and drove along the narrow road from the airport to town. When they were less than five minutes away from the airport, Jim's phone rang. He grabbed it but instantly handed the phone to Morgan, who answered.

"Hello, Mr. Stillwater? This is Ambassador Lofftree."

"Yes, Ambassador, I'm a friend of Jim's. He's driving us to the hotel now. Is there any news about Gwen?"

"Not specifically, but this could be important, and in fact, I find it encouraging."

Jim pulled off to the side of the road, and Morgan handed him the phone. "Ambassador, this is Jim. So, there is something new?" he inquired excitedly.

"As I mentioned to your friend, it's nothing specific, but it does seem encouraging. The coast guard found a line with a nylon collection bag tied to one end of it and an orange float attached to the other less than a mile from where your wife and her friend were diving. Inside the collection bag was a plastic ziplock bag on which someone had written the number two, an x, and the word 'dhow.' Coincidentally, all of the pirate activity has been done using dhows with large outboard motors. We showed the float and line to the captain, and he admitted that it was his and that he had told his mate to cut the line when he ran from what he says were pirates who began to chase and shoot at him. He said that he left both divers behind when he escaped from the pirates, and that is when he fired his shotgun."

"And do you believe him?" Jim asked.

"The coast guard does, and they have released him, but since the mate seems to have taken off, there is nobody to corroborate his story. They did find one piece of evidence on the boat when they gave it a thorough going-over. There was shattered fiberglass near the helm that makes it look like someone shot at the boat from behind."

"So why didn't the captain tell us all of this in the beginning?" Jim wondered, more than a little frustrated.

"The captain said that since he didn't know whether he had hit anyone when he shot back, he was worried about being prosecuted—or worse yet, having the pirates come after him for revenge if the story got out and he was identified. It actually kind of makes sense in this part of the world."

"I guess so. Still, I want to talk to this guy personally," Jim said adamantly.

"I don't think that's a good idea, Mr. Stillwater," the ambassador said.

Morgan had the gist of the conversation, having heard Jim's side of it, so she held out her left hand for the phone while motioning for Jim to give it to her with her right hand.

Jim looked exasperated but handed her the phone.

"Ambassador, hello. My name is Morgan, and as I mentioned, I'm a friend of Jim's. I'm also a coworker, and I came along to offer my support because I was a special agent in federal law enforcement before I joined Jim's company. I can guarantee you that I will help keep things under control, and I may be able to gain some additional information if I have the opportunity to speak with the captain too."

"All right, Morgan, I will see what I can arrange. You must be a good friend to have come all this way to help. I look forward to meeting you."

"Thank you, Ambassador. We will call you back once we get settled," Morgan said before ending the call and handing the phone back to Jim.

"That is good news. Sounds like Gwen and Tanya were trying to tell us who took them but didn't have much time," Jim said.

"That was a real heads-up move, whichever one of them did it. I'll bet we get a ransom demand soon," Morgan said as Jim pulled back onto the road and continued the drive to the hotel.

"The hotel should be on the right before we get into town," Morgan said as she found the Concha Do Mar hotel on the map.

Within minutes, they arrived at the hotel. Situated on the beach, the Concha Do Mar was a sprawling two-story complex of pools, tennis courts, a beach club, and a fishing pier. The long palm-tree-lined driveway led to the main building of the hotel. Doormen hustled to the car to extract Jim and Morgan's luggage while the valet ran up to Jim as he got out of the car and handed him a receipt in exchange for the key. The hotel lobby was well lit, and the freshly painted yellow walls and ceilings highlighted the bright sun coming through the skylights.

"This place looks brand-new," Morgan commented.

"Not what I was expecting, considering that this is one of the oldest hotels on the island according to the tour book," Jim replied.

The check-in was rapid, and Jim and Morgan were directed to the front of the hotel, where a bellman was waiting in a golf cart with their luggage.

"Please," the bellman directed Morgan and Jim to get into the cart. "My name is Pepe. Would you like a tour of the property, or would you prefer to go straight to your rooms?" he asked in heavily accented English.

Jim and Morgan looked at each other and nodded in agreement. There was a canopy to shade them from the hot tropical sun, and the motion of the cart would generate a slight breeze on what had become a sweltering day.

"Yes, a tour would be great," Jim replied as the bellman's face beamed with a seemingly genuine smile.

The tour made the rounds of the property, and the bellman pointed out the many bars and pools and the entrance to the beach club before stopping at a two-story building beside the beach club.

"There don't seem to be many guests here today—the pools are almost empty," Morgan observed.

"It is the off-season, since it is summer in Europe and North America. We do have several families from Argentina and Chile staying here this week," the bellman said as he pulled their bags out of the cart. "This is where you will both be staying. Your rooms are right next to each other, and there is a doorway between them that can be locked on both sides," he said with a grin and wink for Jim. "Follow me, and I will take you to your rooms."

It was a short walk to the elevator for the fleeting lift to the second-floor rooms whose balconies faced the ocean. Morgan and Jim had started to settle into their rooms when Jim's phone rang. Jim saw that it was Hans.

"It's me, and I'm here," Hans exclaimed when Jim answered the phone.

"Glad you made it in OK. Morgan and I were just getting settled into our rooms. The place is really nice. The ambassador rents a suite here in the main building, and we are all invited to join her and her husband for drinks at five o'clock."

"Ah, it's five o'clock somewhere. I'll meet you at the hotel bar at 1600 and bring you up to speed on what I learned from my friend in Lagos before we meet the ambassador. I'm walking to my car now, so I should be checked in and into my room no later than 1530. It's kinda warm here, you know," Hans added.

"It is technically equatorial Africa, and it is July," Jim said matter-of-factly. "Meeting at 1530 sounds good. The bar in the main building where you check in is air conditioned too. I'll let Morgan know," he finished, effectively ending the conversation.

As soon as he got off the phone with Hans, Jim gave Morgan a quick heads-up and got cleaned up for drinks and dinner. He met Morgan in front of their building at 1550, and the two were just starting to stroll over to the main building via a meandering garden path when they noticed Hans heading to the main building from an adjacent outbuilding.

"I guess Hans is staying in another building," Jim said, gesturing in Hans's direction.

Morgan just shrugged.

In less than five minutes, they arrived at the bar and saw that Hans had already grabbed a table near the far end of the room.

Hans jumped to his feet and walked over to greet them when he saw Jim and Morgan enter the bar. "I ordered us bottled water and Glenmorangie. It should be here in a minute. How ya holding up, Jim? Any more news?"

"I spoke with the ambassador on the phone when we got in, and the São Tomé Coast Guard found the tag line from the dive boat with either Gwen's or Tanya's collection bag tied to it. There was a note inside a ziplock bag that said 'two x dhows,' so we're guessing they were picked up in the dhows. Sounds even more like pirates, which is actually encouraging."

"That is encouraging. Any chance that you can take a look and see whether you recognize the handwriting?" Hans asked.

"When we meet with the ambassador, I'll certainly ask," Jim said as Hans led the way back to the table he had staked out for them.

"Long time no see," Hans said as he gave Morgan a hug before pulling her chair out for her to sit down.

"You look good, Hans. I'll bet this weather is a change from New Hampshire's."

"It is at that, a lot hotter than New Hampshire, but the heat's not quite as bad as in Baghdad, and the company is better since you arrived," Hans flirted.

"So, what did you pick up in Lagos?" Jim asked, anxious to gain any tidbit of information that might help him find Gwen.

"Well, it turns out that even though Griz is the head of security for the oil company with the contract for the oil in the Gulf of Guinea, the president of Nigeria is working with a retired US General O'Finn, whose mercenaries are supposed to deal with the security of the oil infrastructure and the piracy issue. They had the pirates beaten back for a few years, but all of a sudden, just about anyone who isn't working for the Nigerian government who wanders anywhere near the oil fields is getting picked up and ransomed. Griz suspects that it might be the mercs doing the kidnapping to supplement their income. He said that this all started about the same time that O'Finn started hiring mostly Russians instead of former British SAS and French Foreign Legion guys."

"Interesting. I had heard that O'Finn was working with the Russians but had no idea he had a contract with the Nigerians," Jim answered.

"So you know this guy," Morgan said, incredulous.

"I know of him. Met him professionally a couple of times and sized him up as a self-promoting asshole, so I'm not a bit surprised that he's working with the Russians or the Nigerians."

"Griz doesn't think much of him either. But here's the interesting part: several of Griz's employees have mentioned to him that they don't believe all of these Russians are actually *former* Spetsnaz," Hans added.

"That part doesn't surprise me either. We were concerned about their posing as athletes and such when I was still a fed," Morgan disclosed.

"To be fair, many of the guys who go into SOF are pretty amazing athletes, and they do compete internationally in many cases, so it may not be as sinister as it sounds," Jim said.

"Yeah, maybe—but think about it," Morgan exclaimed. "Nigeria provides most of the West's light sweet crude. If the Russians controlled Nigerian oil, it would put Europe in a bind and help prop up Russian oil prices. You have mentioned more than once seeing all of the Chinese oil workers in Sudan, so maybe they're just trying to keep up with China."

"Maybe, but in that case, the Chinese oil companies have the contracts," Hans replied.

"So maybe the long-term plan is to change that?" Morgan conjectured.

The waiter, in a shirt and tie, carried over a tray with three glasses and bottles of water. He placed the glasses on napkins on the table and politely asked if there was anything else.

"On that note, let me raise a glass and get back to why we're here. To the return of Gwen and Tanya," Hans said as the three raised their glasses.

For a moment, tears started to well up in Jim's eyes. "I think I need some ice in that in this heat," he said to cover his grief.

"If we can't find her, nobody can," Morgan said reassuringly as she gave Jim a pat on the arm.

The three friends finished their whiskeys and bottles of water, and at five minutes till five, decided to head up to the ambassador's suite. As the three got off the elevator, they were greeted by two Department of State security officers in civilian paramilitary dress with noticeable bulges that pronounced their large barely concealed handguns.

One of the men stepped forward. "Can I help you three?" he asked politely.

"Yes, we are here to see Ambassador Lofftree," Jim replied.

"Can I see some ID, please?"

The three provided IDs. After the security officer had given them a quick look, he nodded to the other officer, who then knocked on the door of the suite. A tall, fit, and friendly-looking man with gray hair answered the door, and the security officer announced the three guests.

"Please come in. I'm Brad Lofftree. Can I offer you some drinks? The room came stocked with some very good gin and local rum."

"Rum and Coke?" Jim asked.

"Absolutely."

"Gin straight up for me," Morgan added.

"Rum straight up for me," Hans put in.

"So, Mr. Stillwater, I understand that you grew up in Miami. Would you like a slice of lime to make it a real cuba libre?" Brad asked as he poured the drinks.

"In fact, I would. Sounds like you've been doing some research," Jim prompted.

"Disappearances always raise lots of questions. There is some concern that Gwen was taken by someone related to your past employment. We think, however, that in cases like that, the parties tend to send a more direct message, and a disappearance does not fit that motive. Do you agree?"

"I do," Jim said, and Morgan nodded in agreement.

Brad had just finished handing out drinks when Ambassador Lofftree entered the room. She was tall, slender, and blond and was wearing a long sundress and sandals. She was stunning. Jim was surprised for a moment by how young she appeared, but as she stepped closer, hints of a more mature woman were revealed, and Jim judged that she too was close to fifty.

"It is such a pleasure to meet you and your friends, Mr. Stillwater. Your reputations precede you all. That said, I am sure that your old way of getting things done won't be necessary here. The São

Toméans are proving to be exceptionally cooperative. Please sit down," the ambassador said as she gestured toward a ring of leather couches in a pit beneath a revolving ceiling fan.

"Thank you, Ambassador," Jim said as he sat down across from her, flanked by Morgan and Hans.

"Please call me Christine. I just now got off the phone, and the boat captain has agreed to meet with you at three o'clock tomorrow afternoon at the coast guard's office at the port. There will be a São Toméan Coast Guard officer present, and I plan to attend as well. Will that fit your schedule?"

"Yes, that will be fine. Any other word?" Jim asked.

"No, not yet. I do have your cell number and will call you night or day if I hear anything new. I know this must be very difficult for you," Christine said sincerely.

"Yes, I admit that it is."

"Well, hopefully you can find some time to relax a bit," Brad added warmly. "This is a beautiful place, and it is the off-season."

"Yes, I hope so. Thank you. The bellman mentioned that it's the off-season and that there are a few families from South America staying here, but other than that, the hotel is nearly empty," Jim replied.

"Yes, South Americans—since it is winter there—and strangely, Russians," Christine said with a small frown.

"Russians?" Morgan said, surprised.

"Yes. About a year ago, the oil workers from Nigeria started coming here for R&R. The hotel loves it since the Russians' bar bills are so high, but it has brought some problems," Christine answered.

"Let me guess: prostitution, gambling, and drugs," Hans said sarcastically.

"Yes, all those. The São Toméan authorities have had their hands full, but the amount of money that is coming in has encouraged many here to turn a blind eye to the corruption as long as it does not affect the locals."

"That's a familiar story. Sounds like the Caribbean—with different bad guys," Jim said.

"Yes, I'm afraid so. In any case, avoid them, and you won't have any problems," Christine advised as she handed Jim an envelope. "I do apologize that I cannot invite you to dinner. I am dining with the São Toméan president tonight, but when I mentioned my reason for coming out of cycle, the president asked me to offer you his condolences and arranged for a complimentary dinner and drinks for the three of you at his favorite restaurant. They will have a table reserved for you all evening, so please, if you do decide to take advantage of his hospitality, you can arrive whenever it suits you. I believe they are open until at least two o'clock."

"Thank you very much, and please pass along my thanks to the president. That was very considerate of him. I am sure that you will both need some time to get ready for dinner, so we should probably get going," Jim said, about to rise.

"Nonsense. São Tomé is very informal, and Christine and I are going exactly as we are now. So I am sure that you all have time for another drink," Brad said as he got up.

"Of course we do," Hans answered before Jim could say anything.

"I was hoping you would. I think we may all have some common acquaintances. I worked with Griz in Mogadishu, and he sent me a note saying that you were a friend of his and would be arriving with Jim," Brad said as he fixed another round of drinks.

"Yeah, Griz has landed himself a nice job," Hans said appreciatively.

"He sure has. No wonder he hasn't retired back to those West Virginia hills that he talks about so fondly. And Jim, we just missed each other in Hawaii. They were still telling stories about you at the detachment when I arrived in November."

"I left in August, and the heads were still rolling over that fiasco in Japan," Jim said.

"Well, you left me with a good bunch of guys, and the bad ones were long gone thanks to you."

"Where did you end up staying while you were there?" Jim asked.

"We had an apartment down in Honolulu, near Punchbowl. I heard about that party house you had in Waiawa. The guys in the det missed it as much as you must have."

"That was a great place to come home to after all of the deployments we had. Can't say I miss that part of it. Gwen loved the place too," Jim said in a suddenly somber tone.

"We'll find her, Jim," Christine chimed in.

"I know we will. I appreciate all of your help," Jim said, looking around the room.

"So, all three of you were army officers?" Morgan asked, somewhat surprised.

"Those two were army, I was air force, but it was all in the same line of work," Brad informed her.

"I still don't know about half the places he went while he was working with guys like these," Christine said to Morgan as she nodded toward Jim and Hans.

"You know about most of them," Brad reassured her.

"I guess I shouldn't be surprised. This is not the kind of place most people go, even under good circumstances," Morgan said.

"Very true," Hans replied. "And with that thought in mind, here's to Gwen and Tanya—and to the Africa Hands in the room who will no doubt find them," Hans added, using the insiders' term of intelligence officers specializing in Africa.

"Cheers," was the reply all around.

After the second round of drinks, Jim, Morgan, and Hans excused themselves and coordinated their upcoming visit to the coast guard office to meet the dive boat captain. The three then made their way to the hotel lobby and sat down on couches in a quiet section of the spacious room.

"They seem like nice people," Hans said to the group.

"Yes, very genuine, and it is a nice surprise that they have some understanding of your background," Morgan said to Jim.

"That is encouraging," Jim admitted as he opened the letter from the president of São Tomé.

"Well, what does it say?" Morgan asked impatiently.

"I am so sorry to hear about the disappearance of your wife and her diving companion," Jim read. "Rest assured we will do everything possible to find her. Please accept an evening of dinner and drinks at my favorite restaurant while you are here. Provide the enclosed card to any cabdriver, and you will be taken to the restaurant. The driver will wait for you until you are ready to depart, at no cost to you."

"Wow, that was really nice of him," Hans exclaimed.

"It certainly was. It would be insulting not to take advantage of it, so let's go before it gets too late," Jim suggested.

"I need to hit the ladies' room first," Morgan said as she got up.

"I think it's over behind the lobby bar," Jim said helpfully, pointing.

"OK, thanks. I'll be right back," Morgan said as she headed toward the bar. Two exceptionally fit men who appeared to be in their thirties gave her a slow look up and down from their barstools as she approached the bar. Morgan avoided eye contact with the men but was within six feet of them as she walked by on her way to the ladies' room.

As she passed, one man said to his companion in Russian, "She is one of the three we are supposed to keep an eye on."

"That part won't be hard—she is one fine-looking bitch," the second man replied in Russian.

Morgan understood every word but gave no hint of it as she continued to the ladies' room without changing her stride. Minutes later, she rendezvoused with Jim and Hans near the front door of the hotel, and they jumped into the first available cab. Jim provided the driver with the card written in Portuguese as the president had instructed, and the cab driver's eyes grew wide for a moment before he had finished reading the card. As he continued reading it, his face erupted into a smile when he realized that he would be paid for the evening and would not have to do much driving.

The restaurant was less than fifteen minutes away, and upon arrival, the cab driver accompanied the three friends into the very high-end restaurant and showed the card to the maître d'. A waiter then stepped forward upon the cue from the maître d'.

"Mr. Stillwater, we have been expecting you and your party. Please follow me," he said in perfect English as he led them to a table with a placard that said *reserved* in Portuguese.

"I feel a little underdressed here," Morgan whispered to Jim as they followed the waiter to their table.

Once they were seated, the waiter placed menus in front of each of them and took their drink orders before informing them of the specials, which were Argentine steak and *arroz de marisco*. "The arroz de marisco is a Portuguese version of paella, and our chef's version is the president's favorite," the waiter said proudly.

"Well, no more needs to be said then. As his guest, I would be honored to try the president's favorite," Jim said.

Morgan and Hans agreed, and all three ordered the same.

"Since you are all having the same thing, may I serve the main course family style? That way you will get an order that is intended for four, and you can pick more of your favorite types of seafood," the waiter suggested.

"That sounds wonderful," Morgan quickly answered for the table.

"Very good. I will bring your drinks and a Portuguese appetizer sampler with some of our very special homemade Portuguese sausage included."

As soon as the waiter departed, Morgan leaned forward, and both Hans and Jim took the cue and leaned forward to listen. "Back at the hotel, two Russians were sitting at the bar, and they were there to keep tabs on us," Morgan told them in an urgent whisper.

"How do you know that?" Jim asked skeptically, whispering too.

"They said so in Russian as I went by. They obviously didn't know that I am fluent in Russian," Morgan said proudly.

"So, are they spotters for kidnapping, or are they involved in the disappearance of Gwen and Tanya?" Hans asked.

"Could be either of those scenarios, or they could be working for the São Tomé president or even Christine. Lots of possibilities here. Good lead, though. Morgan, can you find out who they are?" Jim asked, still whispering.

"If they're at the bar when we get back, I'll give it my best. You two just give me some top cover, OK?"

"How about you let me work on them first? I've been dealing with Russians in Eastern Europe and can get them well on their way to a stupor before I check out and you put on the charm offensive," Hans suggested.

"OK, that sounds good. So, Jim will be stuck with top cover for both of us," Morgan said.

"I have a better idea: we go with your plan, but I invite Brad down for drinks. That will give us an ace in the hole if things go badly and the authorities get involved," Jim said as the waiter arrived with their drinks.

"I can't wait to try the rice and seafood," Morgan said excitedly as the waiter passed out the drinks.

"Yes, I'm starving," Jim exclaimed.

"Your appetizers will be here momentarily," the waiter said politely.

"Ah, guys, we may need to change our plans," Morgan said urgently as the waiter left the table. "Those two men talking to the maître d' are the two Russians from the hotel."

"They seem to be arguing with him," Hans added.

"They probably don't have reservations, which rules out the scenario that they are working for the president," Jim whispered.

"True," Morgan replied.

"They have probably had problems with the Russian oil workers and don't want them in here," Hans added.

"Shit, check this out. The maître d' looks like he's calling the cops. The guy on the right had started to pull out a pistol before the guy on the left stopped him and pushed him out the door," Jim said in amazement.

"Well, at least we know what we're dealing with," Hans said.

"So, are we sticking with the plan if they are back at the hotel?" Morgan asked.

"I think so. I could use a gun anyhow, and I don't think that guy will report it as stolen to the cops if it goes missing," Jim said with a big smile.

"You scare me at times, Mr. Stillwater," Hans said, shaking his head in disbelief.

The appetizers arrived, and Jim ordered two bottles of Vinho Verde to go with the seafood.

"Jim, what's our plan for dealing with the dive boat captain tomorrow?" Morgan asked.

"I'm glad you asked. While you were napping this afternoon, I got in touch with the hotel concierge and arranged a dive trip, with equipment for the three of us, on Captain Rodrigues's boat."

"That is an interesting plan, but there is one problem, Jim: I don't dive," Hans said skeptically.

"I was counting on that. I need you keeping tabs on the captain while Morgan and I dive the site where Gwen and Tanya went missing. I expect that we'll have an interesting discussion with the captain after we have left the port and let him know who we are," Jim said with a ruthless smile.

"That sounds like a dangerous plan," Hans cautioned.

"And getting Russian Spetsnaz drunk and stealing their guns doesn't?" Morgan asked incredulously. "You know, Joe gave me time off to come on this trip specifically to convince you not to try and pull off shit like this," she scolded.

"I know, but you want to do this as much as I do," Jim replied playfully.

"He's right. And what else would you expect him to do?" Hans asked.

"I understand," is all Morgan said as she took another bite of langoustine and washed it down with a sip of wine.

After an hour of continued plotting and sampling the Portuguese delicacies, the main course arrived. The arroz de marisco was exquisite, and plate after plate of delicious seafood was served from the communal pot. The food was as amazing as the service, and after a three-hour feast, the three friends bid farewell to their waiter and summoned their waiting ride.

Jim noticed a small sports car pull onto the road and start tailing them about a quarter of a mile from the restaurant. His instincts were spot-on, since the trailing car turned to follow them up the long hotel entryway and, in a clumsy attempt to keep track of them, pulled in right behind them for valet parking.

Morgan smirked when she saw how awkward the tail was and promptly led the way to the empty hotel bar. The three friends sat down at the three barstools closest to the front door and watched the two Russians, both sporting crew cuts, as they awkwardly followed them in and sat at the opposite end of the bar.

Hans followed the prearranged plan, and after waiting until the Russians had ordered their first drinks, he got up and walked over to the two men. Startled, the man closer to Hans jumped off his barstool. Hans noticed the second man reach under his jacket and rest his hand on the gun in his waistband.

"Good evening. I noticed you guys at the restaurant a little while ago and heard you speaking what sounded like Russian," Hans said pleasantly.

"Yes," the standing man said defensively while the second man remained silent and maintained his seat, his hand still on his weapon.

"I thought so!" Hans exclaimed with a big smile.

"Why—do you speak Russian?" the first man asked, still a little defensive.

"Oh no, just a few words that I picked up in the army. But I have visited Russia and had a really fun time."

"So you are a soldier?" the man said, curiously now. "What words did they teach you?"

"*Vodka, comrade,* and *stoy*!" Hans said sharply, emphasizing *stoy*, the word for *halt*.

Both men laughed, and the second man, still sitting, joined the conversation. "I think we learned more English in our army than you learned Russian in yours," he said with a chuckle.

"Ah, so you're soldiers on vacation. I thought you looked military. Can I buy you a drink, soldier to soldier?" Hans asked.

"You are still a soldier?" the man said suspiciously, noticing Hans's hair and mustache.

"Not anymore; I'm just a veteran. How about you two? You look young enough to still be in."

"No, just veterans. Oil workers now," the man answered, glancing quickly at his companion to make sure that he was listening.

"Even better. Vet to vet. Can I buy you a drink?"

"Da, sure, but the vodka sucks here," the standing man said, now smiling genuinely for the first time.

Hans motioned for the bartender, and he attentively hurried over. Hans ordered a round of vodka and sat down on the barstool next to the standing Russian.

When the man sat back down, Hans introduced himself, and the Russian sitting next to him reciprocated. "I am Dimitri, and this is Serge," he announced. "Those are your friends? Husband and wife?" Dimitri asked, indicating Jim and Morgan.

"Oh no, just old friends on vacation. And she is single if that is what you're getting at," Hans said with a knowing smile.

"She is veteran too?" Serge asked.

"No, she was a cop," Hans responded.

"Cop? You mean police?" the man said, clearly surprised.

"Yeah, but not anymore." Hans nodded in thanks as the three vodkas arrived. He picked his up and held it out for a toast. "To veterans in every country," he said before downing the entire glass.

The two Russians looked momentarily surprised but repeated the toast and downed their glasses too.

"You drink like a Russian," Serge exclaimed.

"I learned that while I was vacationing in Saint Petersburg," Hans said sincerely.

"Ah, so do your friends want to join us?" Dimitri asked.

"I don't think so. I think that my friend is trying to get into her pants, if you know what I mean," Hans said with a wink.

"I don't blame him," Dimitri said and nodded approvingly as he glanced down the bar at Morgan. "OK, it's cheaper that way anyhow. This round is on me." He pointed at the empty glasses and motioned for the bartender to bring another round, which the man promptly delivered.

Serge raised his glass for a toast. "To the Russian army," he said before chugging down his drink, and then he focused his attention on Hans to see if he would repeat the toast.

"To the Russian army," Hans replied and downed his vodka.

Serge and Dimitri smiled.

"Now, to be fair, we need to toast the American army," Hans scolded playfully.

"OK, OK, but only if you buy it," Serge played along.

Hans smiled and waved for the bartender to bring a third round.

Morgan had been keeping track of the number of rounds, and as the third round was consumed with a toast to the American army, she patted Jim on the hand and climbed off the barstool. "Looks like I'm up at bat," she whispered before she started a slow suggestive walk over to Hans.

"Hey, the pretty one is coming over. Maybe she would rather have a Russian soldier in her pants," Dimitri whispered loudly to Hans.

"You mean a Russian veteran?" Hans corrected.

"Oh, yes, a Russian veteran," Dimitri said a bit nervously.

Morgan jumped onto the barstool next to Hans. "I heard you toasting the American army and had to come join you. My name is Morgan," she said, introducing herself to Dimitri and Serge.

"I am Dimitri, and this is Serge. Your friend Hans said that you used to be a cop?"

"Yes, I was, and before that I was an MP in the US Army," Morgan said proudly.

"I forgot about your being an MP," Hans lied.

"I did that for only five years. Are you guys in the army? You look in good shape, like soldiers," Morgan said in an attempt to flatter the men.

"We are veterans. Also oil workers," Dimitri said.

"I gotta take a leak," Hans said suddenly as he stood up and headed for the restroom.

Morgan moved onto Hans's vacated stool, next to Dimitri.

"Now we need to toast the Russian army and the American army all over again," Dimitri said, having calculated that he could get Morgan tipsy in no time, based on her slender build.

"I was hoping you would say that. But can I have a vodka martini?" Morgan asked innocently.

"OK, that's still vodka, but the vodka is not very good here," Serge said, attempting to enter the conversation.

"That only matters for the first couple of drinks," Morgan joked as Serge ordered their drinks.

"Your friend over there looks sad," Dimitri said as he gestured toward Jim. "Maybe he is sad that you would rather sit with two Russian soldiers," Dimitri slipped again, just as Hans returned to the bar.

Morgan started to slowly get up, turning to Hans. "Hans, Jim looks a little sad. Can you cheer him up while I have a quick drink with Dimitri and Serge? I would invite him over, but he doesn't like Russians very much," she confided to Dimitri.

"He doesn't like Russians? Well, to hell with him then. But you like Russians?" Dimitri asked.

"I love Russians, if you know what I mean," Morgan said flirtatiously.

Dimitri and Serge chuckled darkly as their fourth round of vodka and Morgan's martini arrived.

"To Mother Russia," Serge said before gulping down his vodka.

"To Mother Russia," Morgan and Dimitri replied as Dimitri gulped down his vodka and Morgan drank down almost a third of her martini.

"Serge, shame on you. I thought we were going to drink to the Russian army and the American army," Morgan scolded mockingly.

"Oh, yes. So we need more drinks then," Serge said loudly to a skeptical-looking bartender. "Come on, bartender. More vodka," Morgan waved off a refill when she caught the bartender's eye.

The fifth and sixth rounds were having the desired effect, as Morgan noticed that both Dimitri and Serge were getting loud and sloppy. She wondered how many drinks they had had earlier in the evening as she leaned closer to Dimitri, revealing her cleavage and allowing her long hair to brush his arm. She whispered in his ear, "Your friend stares at me a lot, but he's not brave enough to talk very much. Maybe you can convince him to go back to his room before he gets too drunk."

"He is not a brave Russian man like me who can hold his vodka. The problem is we are sharing same room, so maybe you and I go to the room and have more drinks. We leave him here instead," Dimitri whispered back, obviously inebriated.

"I want to stay here a bit longer, then maybe we can go to my room for drinks," Morgan said seductively. "I'll ask Hans to help your friend get to his room, and we can stay here a bit longer, OK?" She motioned for Hans to come over.

"Good idea, Morgan. I think we will be good friends," Dimitri said seriously before turning to Serge. "Serge, you go back to the room. I'll see you tomorrow," he told the man dismissively.

"Not done drinking yet," Serge replied indignantly as Hans came up to them.

"Hey, Serge, let's go to the pool bar on the way back to our rooms and have some drinks there."

"That's a good idea," Dimitri said to encourage Serge.

Serge reluctantly got up, and Hans led the way through the back door of the lobby, fairly certain that he would be able to obtain Serge's handgun before "helping" him get back to his room.

Morgan finished her martini before ordering another and a seventh vodka for Dimitri, who was now leaning heavily on the bar with his elbows. Jim noted that Dimitri was nearly done in, so he paid his tab and waved to Morgan as he exited the bar. Morgan nursed her martini and rubbed on Dimitri's leg, dangerously close to his crotch.

"Dimitri, finish your drink and walk me to my room, OK?"

Dimitri perked up at that, chugged his vodka down, and waved for the check. Morgan watched him sign and noted the room number: 4223. *Building four, second floor*, she thought, memorizing it.

"OK, let's go," Dimitri said as he awkwardly put his arm around Morgan, not expecting her to be taller that he was. The two headed through the door with Morgan steering Dimitri toward the garden walkway to the other buildings.

Just a couple minutes into their walk, Morgan steered Dimitri toward a bench nestled under a tree. "It's so beautiful outside tonight. Let's stop at that bench for a little while," she said.

Dimitri complied without speaking, and the two of them sat down. Morgan put her arms around Dimitri when she noticed Jim sneaking up from behind the bench. She kissed Dimitri and had just moved her head downward as if to kiss his chest when Jim's arm shot out from behind Dimitri and placed the drunken Russian in a sleeper hold, squeezing hard until his body went limp. Jim reached into Dimitri's waistband, retrieving his gun, and Morgan handed Jim her small purse. She waited for a moment for Jim to get out of sight and then started shaking Dimitri in a panic.

"Dimitri, wake up! Wake up! We have been robbed!" Morgan said excitedly.

Dimitri reached for the missing gun and looked suspiciously at Morgan as he regained full consciousness.

"They stole my purse and your gun. Why did you have a gun?" Morgan asked, still excited.

"The gun was for robbers," Dimitri answered groggily.

"Let's call the police," Morgan suggested.

"No police. I got to go find Serge—he has his own gun," Dimitri said as he got up and started to stumble toward building four.

"I'll see you tomorrow," Morgan said before she quickly walked away in the other direction, making for her own building in a round-about route. She finally knocked on Jim's door, and Jim opened it to usher her into the room.

"We have a Glock 17 now," Jim said proudly.

"I wonder if Hans had any luck," Morgan said as there was a knock on the door.

Jim peered through the peephole and opened the door to let Hans into the room.

Hans noticed the Glock on the table and pulled a gun from his waistband. "I guess they were issued Glocks," he said as he removed the magazine, cleared the weapon, and checked on how many rounds he had inside.

"Not a bad night's work. Two guns for the cost of a few drinks," Jim chortled. "We had better hit the sack soon. I want to be the first to get to that dive boat in the morning," he added as he nervously checked his phone for messages again.

"Sounds good," Morgan said. "I'll knock on your door at 0700."

"That works for me," Hans said as he promptly let himself out after having loaded and placed one of the Glocks in his waistband, hidden under his shirt.

"Good night, Jim," Morgan said, giving him a big hug before departing.

CHAPTER 10

SANTO ANTONIO HARBOR, SÃO TOMÉ
11 0830 JULY

Jim and Morgan drove together in Jim's rental while Hans followed in another car. There was no sign of a tail from the hotel, so Jim guessed that Dimitri and Serge were busy accounting for their lost Glocks or getting new ones somehow.

It was another bright, sunny day with no sign of the inevitable afternoon clouds yet. The slight breeze made the morning heat just tolerable.

Jim pulled into a parking spot next to a shack that said *Captain Rodrigues Dive Tours* under a painted red-and-white dive flag. He and Morgan walked up to the open door of the shack holding hands, and Hans caught up to them as a man came out of the shack.

"Hi, we're here on our honeymoon, and we would like to go out to one of the reefs for the morning," Morgan said as she pulled closer to Jim.

"Good morning. I'm Captain Rodrigues."

"Good morning. My name is Morgan, and this is Jim."

"It will be two hundred dollars for the boat and sixty apiece for the rentals and two tanks of air. Are you both certified divers?" the captain asked.

"Yes, Jim is a PADI rescue diver, and I'm advanced open water and wreck certified," Morgan answered.

"You have your cards handy?" Captain Rodrigues prompted. "And how 'bout you? You diving too?" He addressed Hans.

"No, I'm just taking pictures of the happy couple," Hans said with a straight face.

"OK, no problem, but that will be twenty dollars for you for the drinks and snacks. It will get hot when we stop for them to dive, and you will go through a lot of water and sports drinks."

Jim handed the captain $400 and quickly put away his dive card so that the captain wouldn't see his last name.

"OK, you two fill out the paperwork on the clipboards while I get your gear on the boat," Captain Rodrigues said as he went back into the shack to retrieve their gear.

In under twenty minutes, all the gear was loaded, and the captain untied from the dock before starting the engines. "I'm a little shorthanded today; my mate has the day off," he lied.

"That's OK. We're pretty good at getting in and out of the boat on our own," Jim reassured him.

"That's helpful, but I still like to have someone in the back. If you had been brand-new divers, I probably would have sent you down the dock to the competition. Your photographer can help out too, I guess."

"Not a problem. Just tell me what to do if you need something," Hans offered.

The captain maneuvered slowly through the harbor and into the channel, past the last channel marker and No Wake sign. He moved the throttles forward, and the bow of the boat stood up as the two powerful diesel engines were unleashed to speed the vessel forward.

"I'm glad we have some air moving. I was starting to feel kinda funny after smelling that diesel exhaust," Hans said.

"Yeah, it does that to many people," Captain Rodrigues said matter-of-factly as he scanned the horizon. "We don't have far to go."

"Well, that kinda depends. We need to go where you left those two women last week," Jim said, suddenly forceful.

The captain went pale and reduced the throttle, getting ready to turn around.

"We can take all the time we need. You don't have an appointment until three," Jim added.

"Who are you? Is he the husband of the married scientist?" the captain asked, looking to Hans in his panic.

"No, that would be me. We're not really on our honeymoon," Jim answered irritably. "So, do you want to explain to us what happened? Drive straight to their dive site while you're talking."

"You know, piracy is a serious crime," the captain said in a quivering voice.

"You have been paid to take us diving, and that is what we're going to do. My friend Hans is going to stay on the boat to make sure that you don't run off on us too," Jim added.

"He doesn't look like a photographer. I thought something was funny," Captain Rodrigues admitted.

"OK, now look at your GPS, and take us back to where you left Gwen and Tanya," Morgan barked at the captain.

Captain Rodrigues complied and adjusted his course to take them farther offshore. He then recounted the arrival of the pirates and showed them where the bullet had hit to the left of the helm.

"So why did you lie about this? You wasted time when the coast guard could have been chasing the pirates," Jim said angrily.

"I didn't think about that. I thought I might have killed one of them and that they would come back to kill me for revenge," the captain said as he started to sob. "There wasn't anything I could do to help your wife. I am so sorry."

"Well, get us to the dive site," Jim ordered. "They already found the tag line from your boat with a note in it. Maybe there will be something else they left behind on the reef and we'll get lucky."

The seas were calm, and they made good time en route to the dive site, with the captain growing more nervous the farther they went. After more than an hour of tense silence, the captain pulled back on the throttle.

"We're almost there," the captain said, looking at his GPS. "If the pirates come back, we have no way to defend ourselves. The coast guard kept my shotgun," he warned.

"Don't worry, I'll protect you from the pirates," Hans said somewhat mockingly.

"Can you go to the bow and throw out the anchor?" the captain asked the three passengers.

"I got it," Hans responded, and he moved forward as Captain Rodrigues maneuvered the boat with the engines almost at idle now.

As soon as the captain was sure that the anchor was set, he shut off the engines, and the boat started to bob and rock gently from side to side in the one-foot swells.

"The visibility should be to nearly thirty meters in these seas, so maybe you will get lucky and find something," the captain said hopefully. "I'll help you with your gear," he added as he moved to the back of the boat and lowered the wooden dive platform.

In another ten minutes, Jim and Morgan were in the water. After doing a quick buddy check, they were ready to descend, but as they looked full circle around the boat, they noticed that the coral was all bleached white and made the reef look more like a snowscape.

Jim glanced at Morgan as they descended and caught a glimpse of her eyes through her mask, seeing how horrified she looked.

At about twenty-five feet, they were still around ten feet above the reef; heading first to the north, they started to move out in a search pattern for approximately one hundred meters, checking their compasses and counting their kick cycles. They used the boat anchor and line as a base to work from. There was almost no current, which made their search all the more thorough due to the consistent pattern.

After more than thirty minutes of finding nothing significant and seeing very few fish on the barren reef, Jim and Morgan decided to surface.

"Can you believe that? There was almost nothing living down there. I can't imagine Gwen and Tanya taking the time to survey this place," Jim said after pulling the regulator out of his mouth.

"Maybe this isn't the right place? Let's go talk to the captain," Morgan suggested.

"That's a good idea," Jim agreed as he flipped onto his back and started kicking his way to the boat.

Hans was on the dive platform with Captain Rodrigues, and they both helped Jim and Morgan clamber back into the boat.

"There was nothing but bleached coral down there. There weren't even many fish," Jim proclaimed to the captain.

"That's impossible. It was teaming with life just last week! And two weeks ago, I dived here with customers and spearfished, which is why I brought the scientists here. There were some patches of oil on some of the coral, but the contamination was very spotty," Captain Rodrigues said, obviously very puzzled. "Let me double-check the GPS, and then I'll go in with one of you. I keep my gear on the boat, in case of an emergency."

"You can dive with me, but double-check that GPS first while I rest, OK?" Jim responded.

"No problem. Morgan, can you swap his tank while I get my gear?" the captain asked.

"I'm on it," Morgan replied before she pulled a bungee cord over the top of a full tank, removed the tank from the rack along the starboard side of the boat, and swapped it with Jim's half-empty one.

Jim was chugging down his second bottle of Gatorade when he noted that Hans didn't look like he was enjoying the bobbing of the boat. "Hans, jump in and take a swim. It will make you feel better. We have time."

"No, I'm good," Hans said, waving off the idea with his left hand.

"All right, but I used to get a little queasy on rough days, and the cool water made the seasickness go away almost immediately," Jim persisted.

"OK, but watch for sharks, OK?"

"I promise. You'll be in for only a couple minutes, and if you're worried about sharks, just ease into the water and don't splash. We didn't see any sharks anyhow. There are no fish for them to eat."

"Somehow that isn't comforting," Hans said as he slid off the dive platform and into the water, happy to simply tread water beside the boat.

After a few minutes, Jim started getting back into his gear, and Hans crawled back onto the boat looking much better. Jim and Captain Rodrigues went into the water next, and after exchanging OK hand signals, they disappeared below the surface.

In less than fifteen minutes, they resurfaced.

"This has to be the right place. We found the anchor that the captain cut loose last week and tied it off on the anchor line so that we can pull them both back in," Jim yelled from the water to Morgan, who was sitting on the dive platform with her feet in the water.

"How is that even possible?" Morgan yelled back.

In minutes, the two men were back on the boat.

"There is something very wrong here," the captain reflected. "I have been diving in these waters for years and have never seen anything like that. Bleached coral as far as the eye can see."

"And some people don't believe in global warming," Hans said, shaking his head.

"No, this is not warm-water bleaching. That happens slowly. It takes months or even years. This took days. And we have proof that it's the same place—Jim saw how the anchors matched," the captain said emphatically, looking somewhat spooked.

"OK, let's figure this out when we get back to the harbor," Hans suggested gently.

"I'll start pulling up the anchor, or anchors," Morgan volunteered and then moved toward the bow.

"All right, Captain, I believe you. But Hans is right, and we need to get back to meet the ambassador at the coast guard office at three anyhow," Jim said as he removed his equipment and fastened it to the rack behind the bench that ran the length of the boat's rear deck.

Captain Rodrigues stowed his gear in the cabin, grabbed two bottles of red sports drink, and soon had the boat engines started. He took tension off the anchor line, and Morgan got the anchors on board in no time with some last-minute help from the very sick-looking Hans.

"I think you'll feel better when we start moving," Morgan tried to comfort him before he moved back under the awning and into the shade.

"I think I will," Hans agreed, but he was making a disgusted face at the smell of the diesel fumes.

In a little less than two more hours, they were back in port. Jim wanted to check his phone for messages but noticed that his cell battery had died. Jim and Morgan rinsed off under the outdoor showers on the dock while Hans kept an eye on the captain. Hans instructed the captain to ride with him to provide directions to the coast guard office while Jim and Morgan followed in Jim's rental car.

The four arrived more than ten minutes early, but Ambassador Lofftree was already waiting for them. Jim noticed that she seemed very pleased about something, so he hurried over to speak with her.

"Jim, I've been trying to get in touch with you all day! I have some great news. Someone dropped off a ransom demand at the consulate in Lagos. They want to do an exchange in an isolated area between Lagos and Port Harcourt on Saturday the fourteenth. They're asking for two hundred thousand dollars American for each of them, so I guess they understand that scientists don't make a lot of money," the ambassador finished with a broad smile before she gave Jim a big hug.

Morgan hugged him too, and tears started to well up in Jim's eyes for a moment before he managed to compose himself.

"OK, but *I* will make the exchange," Jim announced.

"*We* will make the exchange," Morgan corrected him.

"I'll have the consul general in Lagos support you with transportation. The DEA can help you out too. They have a lot of experience in Port Harcourt," the ambassador added.

"Thank you," Jim said.

"I see that you've already met the captain. Is everything all right, Captain Rodrigues?" the ambassador asked with a worried look.

"Yes, they hired me to do some diving this morning."

"Really? How interesting. Brad told me a little more about your background, so I guess I shouldn't be surprised," she said with a wry smile. "I'll make arrangements for the currency and transportation to Lagos, but you will be billed for the expenses, Jim. Do you understand?"

"Yes, thank you, Ambassador. We'll head back now and get packed up and ready to go. I'll charge my cell phone too," Jim added sheepishly.

"Jim, I just want to apologize once more," the captain said as he headed toward the door.

"Yeah, well, fuck you, Captain. You left my wife to die," Jim said loudly while staring intently into the other man's eyes.

The captain turned and exited.

Morgan put her hand on Jim's shoulder. "We'll get her back, Jim. It's gonna be OK," she said quietly.

"Well, should I invite Dimitri and Serge out for drinks tonight?" Hans said to change the subject and lighten the mood. "We could probably use a few more guns."

"I don't even want to know about that," Ambassador Lofftree said, a little flustered. "I will call you this evening with the travel arrangements, Jim," she added before departing in a sudden hurry.

"Too bad that Brad couldn't make it out last night. He would have enjoyed watching the drunk Russians," Hans said.

"I'll give him a call and see if he wants to head to dinner with us. I'm guessing that the ambassador will not want to be seen with us though." Jim laughed.

"Sounds like a plan. I'll see you two back at the hotel," Hans said as he left the office.

"Hey, don't look now, but Dimitri and Serge are sitting in the parking lot. I think I'll take the long way back to the hotel," Hans declared.

Jim and Morgan glanced at the Russians sitting in their sedan with the motor running; they then looked at each other and just shook their heads and smiled.

CHAPTER 11

NIGER DELTA, NIGERIA
13 0600 JULY

Gwen heard the routine knock on the door of their shack shortly after daybreak.

"Wake up, ladies! It's now time to eat," Mila pronounced loudly in her thick West African accent.

"We are awake!" Tanya yelled back.

"How could anyone sleep with all of these mosquitoes?" Gwen said wearily.

"Ladies, I have some good news for you this morning," another female voice announced from outside the shack.

Gwen pulled on the sandals that her captors had given her and popped out from under the almost-useless mosquito netting. Tanya was already up, having been awakened by the dawn call to prayer, and was doing tai chi in the open corner of the shack. Gwen gave Tanya a quick hug and placed a hand on Tanya's forehead to determine whether she still had a fever that hit her suddenly the day before. As the mother of two, she was very experienced in using her hand to gauge fevers.

Satisfied that the fever wasn't any worse, Gwen moved away from Tanya to pull on the Lycra stinger suit that she had worn on the dive. It provided at least some protection from the mosquitoes. She noticed that the large oil stain on her right arm was now bleached white as if she had spilled Clorox while doing the wash.

"Tanya, didn't you rub up against the coral on the dive and get a big oil stain on your leg?" Gwen asked.

"Yeah, I thought so, but it's kinda funny—yesterday I noticed that the floral pattern on the thigh is bleached white."

"That's what happened to the oil stain on my sleeve. Did someone come get our suits in the night and wash them for us but use too much bleach to get the stains out?" Gwen wondered, incredulous.

"I would ask Mila, but I don't want her to think that we're complaining if they did make the effort to wash our clothes," Tanya said.

"They still smell like seaweed, so I don't think it was them," Gwen said as she finally headed for the door of the hut.

Mila was standing at the door as usual, but she was with another younger West African woman whom Gwen and Tanya had not seen before.

"You still have a fever, by the way, but it seems lower," Gwen said to Tanya as they emerged into the blinding sunlight.

"I do feel better, but I think I'm a little dehydrated," Tanya replied.

"Ladies, why do you look so sad? You get to go home tomorrow," the new woman said cheerily. "But first, we must eat."

Mila started to lead the way to the mess hall but stopped a short distance from the entrance so that the last of the men could leave the building.

"I still don't understand the call to prayer here in the heart of Biafra," Gwen said mildly to Mila as they waited for all the men to depart.

"Johnathan came here from Maiduguri in the north, and while in prison, he learned that the Biafra independence movements in the south hate the government as much as he does. Johnathan also taught us that Islam will provide the discipline we need to overcome our shackles," the new woman said.

"Siri is Johnathan's first wife. She will be escorting you up the coast to where the exchange will take place. You must eat much—there will be little food for you on your journey today," Mila warned as she resumed leading them to the mess hall.

"Nice to meet you, Siri," Tanya said with a faint smile.

Siri looked closely at Tanya as they entered the mess hall. "You are very tall. We need to be sure that the robes will cover you," was her reply.

"Robes?" Gwen asked.

"Yes, you will be in traditional dress, with your faces covered, until we make the exchange," Siri instructed somewhat harshly. "If you remove the robes you are given before then, the guards will treat you appropriately under Islamic law."

"We are not Muslims," Gwen said sharply.

"Today and tomorrow you will be," Siri retorted with a disgusted look, and for a moment, Gwen thought that she was going to spit at her.

"We must get our food now," Mila said as she led the way to the head of the swiftly forming line and motioned for Tanya, Gwen, and Siri to go in front of her.

"Give them plenty," Mila yelled at the servers.

"Last meal," Gwen said sarcastically to Tanya in a low voice.

"That thought did cross my mind—or they're fattening us up to sell us into slavery by the pound," Tanya said in the same sarcastic tone.

CHAPTER 12

LAGOS, NIGERIA
13 1330 JULY

"Thanks for coming along, Brad," Jim said as he, Hans, and Brad piled into the waiting armored Suburban with American diplomatic plates that met them at the Lagos airport.

"No problem, Jim. Damn, it is hot out there," Brad said as he slammed the heavy door shut and wiped perspiration from his forehead.

"Just hope that the AC doesn't break down, sir. These bullet-proof windows don't roll down," Eddie, the young US Marine Corps driver, said with a chuckle.

"If that happens, we'll be safer walking. We would die from the heat in minutes," Jim exclaimed.

"If that happens and you want to walk, just let me know, sir, so I can slow down a little while you jump out. It actually did happen to me and my gunny, and I was thinking the same thing, but gunny and I held the doors wide open until we made it back to the consulate.

I don't think we hit too many people with the open doors." The young marine chortled as he sped past hundreds of pedestrians, who seemed to insist on walking in the road. "So you're here to pay ransom for another tourist?"

"Yep, that's us. But in this case, the tourist is my wife, and the other tourist is her friend," Jim replied curtly.

"Then I'll probably be driving for you guys. I usually get that duty since I raced stock cars before joining the corps," Eddie bragged with a big grin.

"Let's hope we don't need those skills, or things have gone very wrong," Hans answered.

"Too true, sir. I wouldn't worry though. This is a business for these guys, and if they fuck things up, nobody will trust them, so they won't get paid for any more hostages. I have been through this four times now. It always turns out good."

"I'm counting on that, but I'm also ready for the worst—and I have an ace in the hole just in case," Jim said as he stared out the window at the ebbing mass of humanity along the side of the road that went from the airport into the heart of Lagos.

"As soon as we get in, you'll be meeting with the US ambassador to Nigeria and the resident security officer, or RSO. They both flew down from Abuja early this morning. They didn't think you would mind not getting settled in first," the marine said as he swerved hard to avoid hitting a motorbike that had pulled in front of them without warning.

"Fuck me! That guy almost died," Brad exclaimed.

"Yes, sir, and if we hit one, we keep going—or we will end up with a Nigerian necklace. That's when they tie you up, set you in the middle of the road, put a tire over your head, and set it on fire with gasoline," Eddie clarified in a somber tone.

In less than twenty minutes, they pulled into the consulate. Jim noticed that the fenced-in docks across the street from the embassy had several powerboats moored to their pilings. The Suburban was waved into the compound first by Nigerian police officers outside the front gate and then by marines inside the gate. They stopped near the front door of the consulate, and as they opened the heavy armored doors of the vehicle, the heat hit them, and they all reacted almost immediately with severe sweat. The young marine led them inside, past the interior guards and around a metal detector to a small elevator that barely held the four of them.

On the third floor, they nearly tumbled out of the elevator, and the marine led them into the reception area of the consul general's office. A rough-looking woman in her forties glanced up from her computer as they walked in and was just about to say something when the consul general came out of his office and greeted them.

"Good afternoon, Brad, Mr. Stillwater, Colonel Becker. I'm Bob Scanlon, consul general here in Lagos. The ambassador and the RSO are in my office. Please join us," he said as he led them back into his office and introduced them to Ambassador Lance Prepman and Clyde Hardon, the RSO.

The group sat down around a heavy Victorian table that seemed out of place in the otherwise art deco–style office that looked like it belonged in a Miami office park. The ambassador sat at the head of the table.

"Mr. Stillwater, welcome back to Nigeria. First, I understand the stress that this situation is putting you through. That said, I want you to understand that things have changed a lot since you operated here. We have a mature and stable relationship with the Nigerian military that has emerged from the radical Islamic threat that Nigerian institutions are now facing. The decline in the price of oil has also made them much less independent, and their cooperation on a political level has improved. I guess what I'm saying is don't fuck things up, Mr. Stillwater. I have reluctantly agreed to allow you to participate in the ransom exchange but only under the direction of Clyde and his marine guards. Also, please remember that you are a civilian without diplomatic protections. No black passport; no get-out-of-jail-free card. If you break their laws, you will face Nigerian justice, and there won't be a damn thing I can do to help you.

"That goes for both of you too," the ambassador said sternly, pointing at Brad and Hans. "Brad, you do have a black passport, but it has none of the same protections that you have grown accustomed to in São Tomé. You are not a member of my diplomatic team."

"I understand, Ambassador," Brad said.

"Yes, we understand. Can we hear what the plan is now?" Jim said rudely, in a slightly exasperated tone.

The ambassador gestured to Clyde on his left. Clyde stood up, held his hands behind his back, and started to pace next to the table before he spoke. He was a skinny leather-skinned man with the voice of a chain-smoker. "Thank you, Ambassador. Mr. Stillwater, excuse the French, but we have this dicked. We've done this before and quite frankly don't want or need your help. Apparently, someone up the chain thinks a lot of you, so you and your friends will be coming along—unarmed, I might add. But don't worry; my marines will be loaded for bear just in case the shit hits the fan.

"We have the cash in two briefcases and expect a delay while they do a quick count of the first installment and put the money in a shielded bag, as they do know about the trackers. They'll get the second briefcase when we have the hostages back. The exchange will take place down the coast on neutral ground, thanks to an Igbo chief whom we have dealt with in the past. All he asks for in return for setting this up are a few cases of Budweiser. I'll take care of that part too. I suppose you can swim?" Clyde stopped pacing, scanning the three men's faces.

Jim smiled and nodded. Brad and Hans nodded too.

"Good. If shit does hit the fan, get into the water and swim for it. One of our boats will pick you up. I don't expect that to happen, but that's the plan. Most of these guys can't swim worth a shit, and better yet, they shoot worse than they swim," Clyde added as he resumed his back-and-forth pacing.

"So when does this all go down?" Jim asked pointedly.

"Tomorrow at noon, so we'll meet here at the consulate at 0800 for the mission briefing and depart at 0900 on the boats we keep across the street. Eat before you get here, but don't worry about bringing drinking water; we'll have coolers on each of the boats. Any questions?"

"Yeah. When exactly do they release Gwen and Tanya?" Jim asked.

"When we give them the money, one of their boats will *di di mau* away with it while their boss and his security team hang out with us at the village. It's sort of a Mexican standoff until they show up with the hostages about twenty minutes later. They drop the hostages off on the beach, and then they get their black asses back onto their boats, and we don't see them again until the next time," Clyde explained in a seemingly rehearsed response.

"Got it. I guess we'll see you at 0800 tomorrow," Jim said curtly.

The ambassador frowned at Jim and stood up. "I am heading back to Abuja this afternoon. Let my people do their job, Stillwater, and don't fuck this up. Your wife's life depends on it," he said coldly.

Jim stood up too. "I understand," he said as he stared the ambassador straight in the eyes.

"I imagine you will want to get settled in now," the consul general said kindly as he stood up too. "I'll have the marine who picked you up at the airport give you a lift over to the guest quarters. I think you will find them comfortable. There is a decent restaurant, a pool, and several tennis courts if you care to brave the heat and the mosquitoes."

The ambassador departed without another word, followed by the RSO.

"That RSO is a piece of work," Brad said in a low voice to Bob.

"Yeah, I know what you mean. Hey, how's Chris doing? I thought maybe she would tag along," the consul general said, lowering his guard now that the ambassador and the RSO had gone.

"Chris is getting ready for some VIPs from DC, so she headed back to the mainland. She said to pass along her regards, and you should say hi to Sheila for her too," Brad added.

"Maybe we can meet in São Tomé after it cools off a bit. I still haven't made it down there," Bob answered warmly.

"Yes, we should do that. It starts to cool off a bit in October. Can you join us for dinner tonight?" Brad asked.

"Afraid not—other commitments—but have a few drinks for me. Jim, this is going to turn out fine. Just be patient with Clyde. He does know what he's doing, OK?"

"Will do. I guess we'll let you get back to your schedule. Thanks for setting this up for us."

"Don't thank me; thank Brad and Christine. Without them, you would be sitting at home waiting for this to get taken care of."

"I understand. Thank you anyway," Jim said as he walked out of the consul general's office.

The young marine jumped to his feet like he had a spring under him when the consul general entered the reception area. The receptionist continued to ignore everything apart from what was on her computer screen.

"Ready to go, sir?" the marine addressed Jim directly.

"Yep, let's get out of here," Jim replied.

CHAPTER 13

LAGOS, NIGERIA
14 0800 JULY

Despite having drunk at the guesthouse bar with Hans and Brad until long past midnight the night before, Jim woke at dawn as usual. After guzzling several glasses of water, he went to the gym for a brief morning workout. By 0630 he was dressed and headed out to meet Hans and Brad in the restaurant for breakfast. Both were uncharacteristically quiet, but Jim didn't say much either. He wasn't sure whether his companions were simply suffering from hangovers or their planned activities were preoccupying them.

Jim wasn't normally superstitious, but he decided that he didn't want to know if there was something about the day's plan that had these two seasoned combat veterans more worried than usual prior to their mission.

After their quick breakfast, Jim hurried back to his room, pulled an Iridium satcom phone from his bag, and dialed a number from memory.

"Hello?" a familiar female voice answered the phone.

"This is Vette Head," Jim replied, using his old callsign. "We get briefed at 0800, and I should be able to give you the exact location after 0900. The exchange is set for 1200, and they plan to be there early, so figure on two hours east of Lagos, somewhere along the coast. I will text the exact coordinates as soon as I get them," Jim said tersely.

"Got it. Oil Man came through like our friend said he would. I'll get a head start and wait for your call," Morgan replied.

"Sounds great. Out here," Jim ended the call and stuffed the sat-com phone into his backpack before heading back to the restaurant to meet Hans and Brad and wait for their ride to the consulate.

Hans and Brad were both downing more water to make up for the previous night when Jim met them back at their table.

"Did Griz come through?" Hans asked.

"Yes, but I don't have any details. I'll send Morgan the coordinates as soon as I can. She's going to be about thirty minutes ahead of us," Jim whispered.

"Backup plan in place! I love working with you guys," Brad whispered back excitedly.

Their conversation was interrupted by Eddie, who had been sent to pick them up. "All set, gentlemen? I'm sorry I won't get to drive for you later today. Some stupid squid gets to do the driving where you guys are going today," he ended dejectedly.

"Well, at least we'll get to the consulate in one piece. That's never a guarantee around here," Brad reassured him.

LAGOS, NIGERIA 14 0800 JULY

Eddie smiled and led the way to the still-running Suburban parked in front of the guesthouse in the walled guest compound. Everyone piled in, and even the marine was quiet as they navigated the crowded and narrow Lagos streets for twenty minutes to get to the consulate.

Once at the consulate, the marine led the way to a second-floor conference room filled with metal folding chairs. There was an LCD screen at the front of the room with white boards flanking both sides of it. A collection of marines in battle rattle and middle-aged men in cargo pants, polo shirts, and utility vests filled the room.

Jim, Brad, and Hans were the oldest in the room—except for the scrawny RSO—by at least ten years. Everyone took their seats, and an African American man built like a Miami Dolphin and wearing a Drug Enforcement Administration badge embroidered on his black polo shirt stepped to the front of the room. Jim was glad to see George, as he worked with him last time he was in Nigeria. He knew George was as fit as when he played wide receiver in college.

"Good morning. For those of you who don't know me, my name is Special Agent George West. Now, let's get started. Clyde, do you want to kick things off?" George said with a subtle South Florida accent.

The RSO stood up and strutted to the front of the room. He looked around the room to see who was present and wiped his damp, greasy hair straight back with the palm of his hand before speaking. "Thanks, George. Most of us have been through the drill a few times by now, and those who have not need to remember that and stick to the plan we lay out here this morning," Clyde said as he looked straight at Jim, who acknowledged him with a subtle nod.

123

"I have the ransom money prepared in two briefcases. We will hang out on the west side of the tiki huts, where the chief of the village and a few of his men will be. It's about twenty yards from the beach," Clyde said, turning to point at a map of the village. "As you can see, this is a pretty narrow barrier island, so when the kidnappers arrive, they will hang out on the east side and let the chief know when they are ready. When both sides are ready, the chief will head back to his village, and Mr. Stillwater and I will walk to the big tiki hut and wait. When the kidnappers arrive at the tiki hut, we will give them half the money, and then the hostages will arrive in fifteen to twenty minutes. Mr. Stillwater will ID the hostages—which is the only reason why he is accompanying us today—and then we will trade the second briefcase for the hostages while their security team and ours face off. It's gonna be tense for a few minutes, but their security team is surprisingly disciplined. Any questions?"

"Where will our boats be while this is going on?" Hans asked with a slightly troubled look on his face.

"The boats will be in shallow water near my marines on the beach. We have some guys TDY from Little Creek and one navy boat handler will pilot each boat, and they will remain in the boats with the motors running. You and Brad will be in the second boat—and you will stay there. I am well aware of your knowledge in these matters, Stillwater's too, but George and I are running the show. George, you take it from here. You need to get outta here before we do," Clyde finished as he stepped aside and gestured to George.

"Thanks, Clyde," George said as he stepped forward and immediately captured the attention of everyone in the room with his natural charisma. "So, the backup plan is for me and two of my agents to be positioned in the village inside the chief's house. He is not as neutral as he lets on; and he has a safe full of 7.62-millimeter

FN FALs that he will make available to us after we sneak in with a group of villagers coming back from a grocery run to Lagos. Unless something goes wrong, you will never know we are there. The chief will not go to the tiki hut until we are in place. Clear?" George said in a commanding tone as he looked around the room.

The marines in the room shouted back with a loud, "Clear, sir!"

"All right. I need to get moving, and the rest of you leave the dock in thirty minutes," George said as he headed for the door. Two of the seated men in the room jumped up and followed him out.

The rest of those assembled rose to their feet more slowly and herded themselves into groups as they filed through the door. Clyde led the way with the marines behind him, and Jim, Hans, and Brad followed closely behind the marines as they headed down the stairs and out of the consulate toward the docks across the street. Each marine grabbed an M16 from a rifle rack at the guardhouse as they filed past.

"Hey, do we get those too?" Jim joked to the marine monitoring the rifle rack. The guard looked unamused and waved him on.

"What's wrong? Aren't those Sig 9 millimeters I got you guys big enough?" Brad whispered to Jim, who chuckled and patted the pistol hidden under his shirt.

Jim noticed Clyde wave the marines ahead and step behind the guard shack at the front gate of the consulate, his cell phone in hand, just as a white Peugeot 208 with George and his two men inside sped out through the gate to go rendezvous with the villagers' boat a few miles away. Hans pointed to the Peugeot, and Jim nodded, taking the opportunity to reach inside his backpack and text Morgan the coordinates of the ransom exchange. He pulled out a water bottle to make it look like that was what he had been digging into the pack for and sped up his pace to catch up to the marines.

"General, this is Clyde. We are good to go. Just make sure that your men don't decide to count the money at the exchange, since that Boy Scout Stillwater will be with me. I already removed my cut when the DEA guys delivered the money last night."

"Don't worry about that. Just keep Stillwater and his buddies on a tight leash. If they grab any of my boys, it won't be long until someone figures out how you are involved. Do we understand each other?"

"Yes, sir. I'll call back when this is done. Gotta go. Out here," Clyde said as he ended the call abruptly, looked around to see whether anyone was watching him, and jogged out through the gate to catch up with the men assembled on the docks across the street, waiting for word to climb into the boats.

Clyde stepped to the front of the group and yelled, "Listen up! The boat here behind me is boat number one. Stillwater and I will be in this one with the navy boat pilot and two marines in battle rattle. Hans and Brad, you'll be in that boat, boat number two, with those two marines and the navy boat pilot. Understood?"

"Yes, sir!" the marines shouted back in unison.

"All right. Let's load up, and we will get going on time," Clyde shouted.

The groups loaded onto the boats as instructed with one marine on each side of the boat behind the pilot. A civilian attending the docks untied the boats and tossed the lines to the marines as the boats' huge outboard motors started almost simultaneously. Clyde waved his arm and pointed the way forward, and his boat leaped up on plane, with the second boat following close behind.

The day was already steamy hot, so the wind and spray felt good on Jim's face as the boat got up to speed. He felt nervous about the exchange for a moment but immediately put that thought out of his mind, reminding himself that he would see Gwen by noon.

The two boats slowed as they pulled into the main shipping channel at Lagos harbor, following the no-wake rules as they moved past docked freighters flying flags from all around the globe. Cranes on the docks moved almost rhythmically, loading and unloading cargo.

In ten minutes, the boats emerged from the harbor and got back up to speed as they followed the main shipping channel into the Gulf of Guinea and turned east, following the coast. Jim counted more than twenty fishing boats and pondered the possibility that at least one of them might be a lookout boat for the kidnappers. He also hoped that Morgan had gotten a good head start and was well ahead of them.

After another thirty minutes, Clyde pointed to a cluster of tiki huts near the beach. "We're almost there. Oh, I forgot to mention, you are gonna get your feet wet." He chuckled.

Jim wondered whether that had been planned, in case someone was wearing a wire or a tracking device.

The boats slowed to an idle as they gradually nosed their way closer to the white sandy beach. When the water was only a couple of feet deep, the marines scurried across the bow of the boat and jumped into the water. They headed about twenty yards inland and faced the tiki huts at port arms.

"Time to get wet," Clyde said as he jumped in too, carrying the two small briefcases, and jogged up the beach to stand behind the marines. Jim followed closely behind him.

Jim noted that the only cover came from a few coconut trees and the pillars the size of telephone poles that held up the thatched roofs of the tiki huts. By the time he was in place behind the marines, both boats had roared to life and maneuvered into slightly deeper water.

Looking down the beach, Jim could see that the barrier island they were on was less than a mile long, and they were at about the midpoint of the beach. The village was another fifty yards inland, tucked in among more trees. He guessed that the main docks must have been along the protected channel between the island and the mainland.

In less than five minutes, a man in a white tribal robe and a woven cylindrical hat emerged from the village. Two similarly dressed men, each with a FN FAL rifle slung over his shoulders, walked a couple of paces behind him. The chief waved, and Clyde waved back before the chief slowly walked to the largest of four tiki huts and sat down on a bench. The two bodyguards remained standing and faced east, clearly expecting others to arrive. They were apparently not at all concerned about any threat posed by the four armed marines, despite how intimidating those marines looked in their helmets and body armor.

Jim stared first down the beach and then offshore, anticipating the arrival of the kidnappers. He was surprised when instead of arriving from the ocean side, three dhows with throaty outboard motors emerged from behind the island and headed toward them, perilously close to the shore. Just before the boats reached the tiki huts, the engines slowed to idle; a man jumped out of each boat and pulled the boats onto the beach, using lines from the bows, before four more men climbed out of the boats and onto the beach without getting wet. Each of the men had an AKM with folding stock slung across his chest.

The chief waved at the men, and one man waved back to the chief. The chief stood up and headed back to the village with his guards, disappearing into the sea grape trees before two of the kidnappers proceeded to the tiki hut and motioned for Jim and Clyde to join them. Clyde dropped one of the briefcases behind the line of marines and moved forward. Jim walked beside him and noticed that one of the two men in the tiki hut was holding up a cell phone, apparently filming them.

"It is so nice of you to join us this morning in this beautiful spot," the taller man with a gold front tooth greeted them with what Jim recognized as a very proper London accent. The other man was now busy on his cell phone, strangely oblivious.

Clyde handed the briefcase to the man with the gold tooth. The man thanked him and turned to walk back to the rest of his group on the beach. The man with the cell phone suddenly seemed extremely excited as he tapped his companion on the shoulder to get him to hurry.

"We'll wait right here!" Clyde yelled to them.

Jim continued to watch the man with the cell phone, who was becoming increasingly animated as he started to show the other men on the beach whatever he had discovered.

"They must be looking at some pretty hot porn," Clyde joked when he noticed the man showing his cell phone to all of the others.

"Something isn't right," Jim warned.

"Just cool your jets, Stillwater. You former SOF guys are all the same. Don't let your PTSD kick in and fuck this up, or you won't ever see your wife alive again," Clyde returned cuttingly.

"They aren't looking at porn," Jim persisted. "They're looking back and forth between the phone and us."

"Just stay calm. Half of them are gonna disappear with the first half of the money, and your wife is gonna be here in no time," Clyde said somewhat reassuringly, as the man with the gold tooth jumped into one of the dhows; it sped away from them along the shore the same way it had come.

"I need to make a call," Jim announced as he flipped the backpack off his back and pulled out his small satcom phone.

"A call?" Clyde looked skeptical.

Jim punched in the speed dial for Morgan, and she answered almost immediately. "Jim, something isn't right. I had a visual of the kidnappers from the oil company boat, and I know that they did not see me. We watched the kidnappers move down the intracoastal channel behind the barrier islands, and one of the dhows has two very tall women in full robes under guard. They were stopped on the other side of the island, but now they're headed back in the direction they came from, and two of the men in another boat are putting on women's robes."

"Can you catch the boat with Gwen and Tanya in it?" Jim asked excitedly.

"Yes—unless they can get into the mangroves where it's too shallow for us. Griz and his men are armed to the teeth, so we can take them down without any trouble. We're on it," Morgan added.

"This is a setup!" Jim yelled at Clyde.

"I don't know who you were talking to, but this is all going as planned. Now, put the satcom phone on the table, and put your hands on top of your head," Clyde said as he pulled out a Beretta 9 mm and pointed it at Jim with one hand while he answered his cell phone with the other. "Yes? Well, now, that is a nice chunk of change. He has his hands on top of his head. I'll tell the marines that he needs to deliver the other briefcase by boat, since your boys spotted the DEA guys in the village."

Clyde turned to the marines and yelled, "One of you bring me the other briefcase!"

One of the marines ran over with the briefcase.

"This is a setup," Jim warned again. The marine looked confused by the sight of Clyde holding him at gunpoint.

"He is full of shit, and he almost fucked this up by trying to take down the kidnappers all by himself. Now get back to where you were, and wait until they come and get the briefcase."

"What about the hostages, sir?" the marine asked.

"They will be back here in a few minutes after Jim meets them with the money. Now get the fuck back with your marines," Clyde bellowed.

The marine ran back without saying another word and immediately started a lively conversation with the other three marines.

Clyde dialed George's number while keeping the Beretta pointed at Jim. George answered on the first ring. "George, this damn fool hero has decided that he needs to deliver the money by himself, since someone in the village saw you guys arrive this morning and alerted the kidnappers," Clyde lied.

"Don't let him do it. We'll just call this one a day and set up another exchange," George instructed.

"Well, that's what I told him, but I'm not sure he's gonna listen. Let me see if I can talk some sense into him," Clyde said as he ended the call.

"All right, Jimbo. Slowly pick up the suitcase, keep the other hand on your head, and start walking toward those dhows. I will kill you if you try anything, since I can't have you telling your side of the story, now, can I? I don't want to have to kill you though, since you're apparently worth a nice chunk of change if we turn you over to the Dakar Islamic Mujahedeen up north. I think they have big plans for you. You might even get to be the star in your own movie. Now move!" Clyde said as he gestured with the gun.

Jim complied, knowing that Morgan was almost sure to rescue Gwen and Tanya and would have a good idea of where they were going to take him—just in case he couldn't get out of this on his own in the next few minutes.

Jim slowly walked toward the dhows and was about halfway there when two of the kidnappers ran forward. Jim swung the briefcase and caught one of the men across the face with it before flinging it across the beach. The other kidnapper raised his AKM and stuck the muzzle in front of Jim's nose. The first man spit blood and laughed before patting Jim down and finding the Sig in his waistband. He showed the gun off to Jim with a big smile and stuck it into his own belt.

"Get in the boat and lie facedown," the man with the AKM ordered in a strange Cockney accent.

Less than a second later, a shot was fired from the village; it struck the man in the forehead and blew out the back of his head.

Jim jumped on top of the man who had taken his Sig and snapped his neck in a single move; he then froze on top of the body as bullets from an AKM stitched a circular pattern in the sand around him. Another man grabbed him by the backpack and shoved him into the boat while the others returned fire at the village, ignoring the marines who were now running toward one of their boats, which was making its way to shore to pick them up. Another dhow was also racing toward them as its passengers shot at the village.

"Don't shoot at the marines!" the man with the gold tooth yelled from the second dhow. "They are not allowed to shoot at us unless we shoot at them!" he added with a hearty laugh.

The dhow Jim was in pulled away from the beach. Two AKMs were trained on him, and there was no way he could jump out of the moving boat before one of the kidnappers pulled the trigger. Jim knew that it was now all up to Morgan. At least the skirmish on the beach had delayed the two dhows carrying most of the armed men, and the dhow with Gwen and Tanya in it would be a sitting duck when Morgan and Griz's oil company security team caught up to it.

Meanwhile, George and his team moved to the large tiki hut as Clyde and the marines left on their boats.

On the oil company security boat, Morgan had tried several times to get in touch with Jim. When a call was finally answered, she was relieved until a voice that she didn't recognize greeted her. Griz was standing close to her, trying to listen while holding on as the boat raced toward the dhow ahead of them.

"Jim?" Morgan asked.

"This is George, a friend of Jim's. Whom am I speaking with?" George asked politely.

"This is Morgan. Now, where is Jim?" Morgan demanded.

"This is Special Agent George West, DEA. Where are you?"

"Special Agent George West," Morgan said out loud to Griz.

"He's from the embassy," Griz explained to Morgan as he grabbed the phone from her. "George, this is Griz. Sounds like things went to hell in a handbasket. It was some kind of a setup on their side. Looks like they were trying to trade two of their own, and we're chasing the dhow that has the two female hostages right now. We should catch up to them in about two minutes."

"Make quick work of it. There are three more dhows loaded with guys armed with AKMs, and they have Stillwater," George exclaimed.

"Holy shit! How did that happen?"

"I won't know until I debrief the RSO and the marines. I do know that they left behind one dead guy with the back of his head missing thanks to my sniper, but we couldn't get another shot off without hitting Stillwater."

"You might have done him a favor. Seems like they wanted him more than the money," Griz mused.

"Maybe, but they got both and kept the hostages, unless you can fix that. I think—"

George's sentence was rendered inaudible as the M2 Browning "Ma Deuce" on the bow of the security boat fired at close range and obliterated the outboard motors on the dhow ahead, leaving it dead in the water. It instantly started to sink from its many holes.

Gwen and Tanya yanked off their robes and jumped into the water, swimming toward the oil company boat while their three captors swam toward the nearby shore. Two security men with G3s fired at the men in the water, and all three slipped under the surface before they made it to shore.

Griz's security men on the boat threw life preservers into the water, and when Gwen and Tanya reached them, the men pulled the women toward a dive platform at the stern of the boat. Morgan was the first to reach out a hand to Gwen and pull her out of the water as Tanya clambered onto the wooden platform without help.

"I hate to rush you, but they have Jim, and we need to go now!" Morgan yelled.

Everyone scrambled onto the deck of the boat, and the captain immediately pushed to full throttle and sped them back in the opposite direction. Griz looked through binoculars and saw the dhow heading toward them. The occupants of the dhow saw the larger security boat racing toward them at almost the same instant and made a sharp turn for the shore.

The captain slowed and headed to the spot onshore where the dhow was now abandoned. The men had driven onto the roots of the mangroves under full power in their hurry to get away from the security boat.

The gunner on deck with the M2 covered the shoreline while security men loaded into a Zodiac and made their way to shore to inspect the dhow.

"Nothing here, Griz, and no sign of where they went. Those mangroves are really thick, and they could be anywhere," one of the security men called over the radio.

"Make sure they can't use that boat again and get back here. We need to get to the consulate for the debriefing," Griz ordered.

In minutes, the security detail were headed back in the Zodiac, and two explosions from breaching charges cut the wood hulled dhow in half.

Griz called George on the satcom. "Hey, George. We have the hostages except for Stillwater, and we have coordinates for the place where they took him inland. I don't have any of the company helicopters up now, so you had better let the Nigerian military know. And who knows? Maybe they will decide to help out. Are you ready to copy?"

"Go."

"The coordinates are 6°16'06"N and 4°34'08"E. We are headed to the consulate now. See you when we get there. Out here," Griz said as he ended the conversation.

Morgan joined Gwen and Tanya in the cabin of the security boat. The captain was already handing them multiple bottles of sports drink from the cooler on deck.

"So who are these people? Who took Jim?" Morgan asked excitedly.

"They're gonna be dead soon if they took Jim. The only unknown is whether I kill them before he does," Gwen screamed, tears in her eyes.

"They're Islamists who have somehow influenced the Biafra independence movement. They treated us surprisingly well, and we're pretty sure that this is just a money-raising sideshow for them. We watched them training to take over oil rigs, so it looks like they will soon be taking this whole hostage thing to a new level," Tanya explained calmly.

CHAPTER 14

US CONSULATE, LAGOS, NIGERIA
14 1500 JULY

Tanya and Gwen were quickly taken to the airport so they could get medical examinations at Ramstein Air Force Base near Kaiserslautern, Germany. Two FBI special agents experienced in debriefing hostages joined them on the US Air Force C-17.

Everyone else who had been involved in the hostage exchange was herded into the briefing room. They were seated and silent and busy writing down what they had seen, and Special Agent George West assumed complete control. Clyde, as the RSO, sat in the front row, writing out a statement along with everyone else. The room was still eerily dead silent. George had instructed them to write exactly what they had seen and not collaborate. There was a dead Nigerian and a missing American to explain.

Several of the young marines finished quickly. They were literate but not experienced writers, so their statements had few details. Several other marines struggled to put down their words. After George's men were done with their own DEA-6 reports, they pulled the marines into their office one by one and helped them finish their statements.

After almost two hours, everyone had finished, so George collected the statements and addressed the room. "OK, thank you all for your cooperation. This has been a tough day for everyone. We helped two Americans regain their freedom, but we now have a decorated intelligence community veteran in serious jeopardy. We have a lot to do, so this is going to be a long evening and maybe even a long night. That said, we are going to build a timeline of what happened. I have your statements, and if you deviate from those statements as we proceed, you will need to explain why. Let me remind everyone that lying to a federal law enforcement officer is a serious crime. That's what they busted that famous food lady for, so believe it: you will go to jail if you lie to me. Understood?"

The marines responded with their typical loud "Yes, sir!" while everyone else nodded in agreement. The mood was still somber.

A young buck sergeant jumped to his feet. "Sir, request permission to speak, sir."

"Go ahead. What do you want to say, Sergeant?" George said kindly.

"Sir, we could have fucked those guys up bad, but we weren't even allowed to fire, since we weren't fired upon. I feel terrible about letting those ragheads take one of ours," the young man said emotionally.

One of the DEA agents stood up. "Sergeant, I had a sniper rifle with scope, and I only got one clear shot that allowed me to take out one of the bad guys without taking out Stillwater too. Don't beat yourself up about this. The best way to get our man back is to look for clues in what we saw. You may not think it's important, but when we put it together with what other witnesses saw, it might make the difference. Do you understand me, marine?"

"Yes, sir!"

"OK, Sergeant, why don't you start?" the DEA agent said.

"Sir, once we arrived, I put my marines in a line at port arms, facing the tiki hut. Mr. Stillwater and the RSO were standing behind us, since we were wearing full body armor and battle rattle. That Igbo chief showed up with his two bodyguards just as we expected him to. I felt good about that since I knew that the DEA guys must have made it to the village OK. Pretty soon, those goddamned ragheads showed up in three motorboats. The chief acknowledged them and walked back to the village with his bubbas. Then two of the ragheads walked up to the tiki hut while the rest of 'em waited by their boats. The RSO gave the tall guy the first briefcase while the other guy was taking pictures with his cell phone. The guy with the cell phone got real excited all of a sudden and started showing the screen to the rest of his people. Then two other guys left with the briefcase in one of the boats. The next thing I saw was the RSO getting a phone call—"

"I was calling George!" Clyde yelled out.

"Go on, Sergeant," George said as another DEA agent stepped into the room and whispered something into his ear. George frowned and nodded.

"After the RSO got off the phone, I saw Mr. Stillwater pull a sat phone out of his backpack and make a call. After that, the RSO took out his Beretta and pointed it at Mr. Stillwater. Then he yelled that he wanted the second briefcase, so I ran over with it, and Mr. Stillwater said that the deal had gone bad."

"I'm not gonna sit here and listen to these lies!" Clyde blurted.

"It ain't a lie, sir," the marine sergeant replied matter-of-factly.

Clyde stood up and started to head for the door, shoving George out of the way.

George grabbed the RSO by the arm and spun him facedown on the floor. "You are under arrest, Clyde," he said sternly as another DEA agent grabbed Clyde and handcuffed him.

"What the hell for?" Clyde yelled.

"I forgot to mention that we found the second briefcase on the beach, and it was fifteen thousand short. Tim just found the missing fifteen K in your quarters, Clyde," George said disdainfully before he stood back up to address the room. "Everyone else is free to go. We'll go through your statements and get back to you if we have any questions. Our priority now is finding Mr. Stillwater."

"Aren't we gonna finish the timeline, sir?" one of the marines asked.

"No, marine, we are done for now. I was just trying to keep everyone in one place while we sorted some things out." George turned to face Morgan and Hans. "Morgan, Hans, can we speak privately in my office?"

Hans and Morgan followed George to his office, and George pulled a bottle of Jack Daniels and three glasses out of his desk drawer before joining the others at a small meeting table in the corner of the room.

"I'm sorry I don't have any ice; my damn fridge is broken," George apologized as he poured three drinks without asking.

"What's being done to find Jim?" Hans asked.

"Our best shot is pressuring Clyde to tell us who has him, but I think we're going to have an even bigger problem. What I didn't mention before was that we checked Clyde's cell phone too, and right after the mission briefing, he made a call to a retired US general who's doing some security work for the Nigerian government. He also got a call from someone at the tiki hut right before he pulled his gun on Jim. We saw all that from the village with our binoculars. So here's my theory: the guy with the cell phone used some social media site to find out Jim's identity and then ran it through some jihadi site and found out that Jim has a price on his head. One of our intel guys ran his name and in five minutes found that some group called DIM—Dakar Islam Muj or some horseshit name like that—is offering seven hundred K for Stillwater. Did he ever mention that to either of you?"

"No, but it doesn't surprise me. There's a bounty on DEA agents too, I hear," Hans replied.

"So where are these guys? Dakar?" Morgan asked.

"That would be way too logical. Maybe their leader is from there, or maybe they just liked the name. Dakar Rally maybe? At any rate, they are based in Maiduguri. Unlike Boko, they don't live out in the bush; they mainly hang out in mosques, coffeehouses, and Internet cafés."

"Do you have anyone in Maiduguri?" Morgan asked.

"I don't have anyone in place, but the Nigerian Drug Law Enforcement Agency and, of course, the State Security Service both have people there. The Nigerian army has a base there, so I'll ask the attaché if he has any contacts. The problem is that with seven hundred thousand American on the line, there's a lot of room to pay someone off to look the other way."

"So how do we get there?" Hans asked.

"Nigerian Air flies there. You are going to stand out like a sore thumb if you go to Maiduguri, and you might end up getting kidnapped too. I would not recommend it," George warned as he took a sip of Jack Daniels. "That was rude of me. Cheers." He raised his glass and toasted Hans and Morgan.

Morgan downed half the glass in one gulp as Hans took a few small sips.

"I think the best strategy is to find him before he gets to Maiduguri, assuming that is where he's going to end up. He won't be flying, so we might have a little time to get some roadblocks set up," Morgan conjectured.

"They won't set up roadblocks for one American," George said skeptically.

"No, but they might if we spread the word that the head of Boko was headed back up north after a trip south to recruit followers," Morgan said smugly.

"Whoa, whoa, whoa. I can't just make up a report like that and spread it around," George said before he finished his Jack Daniels and promptly poured another.

"You didn't make it up. You heard it from...a walk-in?" Morgan replied. "Yeah, a walk-in source. Me," she added with a grin. "A former law enforcement source with known connections to terror organizations."

Hans shook his head and grinned.

"That just might work," George said as he stood up. He walked over to his desk, picked up the phone, and dialed a number written on a note card under the clear plastic desktop. "General Siska, this is George West. I got a tip that the head of Boko is en route to Maiduguri from down in the delta."

"George, it is very good to hear from you. This is a big coincidence. I heard that there might be a missing American being taken to Maiduguri by some very bad people. Perhaps they are traveling together?"

"Perhaps they are, General," George played along.

"Very well. Based on your important information, I will set up roadblocks along the route, and maybe we will find them both. It is always a pleasure to speak with you. I will be sure to stop in and have a drink with you the next time I am in Lagos. Maybe you can even spare another case of Jack Daniels so that I have some on hand when you come to visit me?"

"That's not a problem, General. Expect it by the end of the week. Thank you, General."

"Thank you, George. Goodbye now," the general said as he ended the call.

Morgan had refilled all three glasses on the table. "Cheers, George," she said as she raised her glass.

"Cheers," Hans and George replied.

"By the way, are you coming with us to Maiduguri? We'll be on the first flight out tomorrow morning," Morgan added.

"What's that saying? In for a penny, in for a pound. Yeah, I'm coming too. I might as well go now and keep you two from getting in trouble with the Nigerian authorities instead of waiting, only to be sent up there tomorrow afternoon to get you out of jail."

"Thanks, George. We appreciate all that you've done," Morgan said sincerely.

"George, one thing that still puzzles me are those fucking Russians. They followed us in São Tomé, so they are involved in this somehow," Hans said, exasperated.

"Well, you are right about them being players, but we're still not sure what they are up to. When O'Finn started hiring more Russians instead of former SAS guys, the heroin trafficking and human trafficking took a big upswing. I had at least five open investigations. That went on for about a year, and the few Russians we were able to get the Nigerians to arrest were washed-up, worn-out, and long-retired Spetsnaz—Russian special forces—from the Afghanistan war. After about a year, though, the Russians who were coming here on O'Finn's contracts were younger and tougher, and although they drank their white Russian asses to sleep every night, there was very little criminal activity."

"When I spoke with Griz about the Russians, he said that some of his men thought that some of the new Russians were not former but active Spetsnaz. Any intel on that?" Hans pressed.

"Goddamn it, Hans, you know that there is a limit on what I can tell you guys. But OK, I will say this: Nigeria has light sweet crude that competes directly with the Russians', and since Nigeria does not follow OPEC limits, the Nigerians keep the price of oil low as long as they pump whatever they want. OPEC and the United States with their shale production are squeezing the shit out of the nouveau commies with low oil prices. On the east coast of Africa, China has already moved in and taken over much of the oil market. The only place left to make a play for control of the oil is Nigeria, so in my humble opinion, that is why the fucking Russians are here. But how will they gain control? Buy it? Threaten it? Or ruin it?" George wondered in a slow, somber tone.

"So why the hell would they keep tabs on us in São Tomé?" Morgan asked. "That part still does not make sense."

"It could be that they were trying to figure out how much money to ask for, or it could be that they made no connection between you and Tanya and Gwen. You were going to be the next nosy tourists to get kidnapped. Sorry to piss on your conspiracy theories about the Russians, but I think that last scenario is most likely," George said.

"Maybe. But maybe there is something that they're trying to protect," Morgan said as she finished her third glass of bourbon.

"George, can you meet us at the guesthouse at 0600?" Hans asked.

"Shit yeah I can, but let's call and make reservations now and get some dinner. My treat, OK?"

"We are going to get Jim back!" Morgan spoke emphatically.

"I know we are," George replied.

CHAPTER 15

DELTA STATE, NIGERIA
15 0600 JULY

The car stopped, and Jim felt the car shift as its occupants exited. The doors slammed shut, and he heard a key being inserted into the lock of the trunk. Cooler air hit his sweat-soaked clothing, and light flooded in as the lid of the trunk was opened. After having spent all night in the trunk without water, Jim was too weak to sit up on his own and stayed on his side with his hands zip-tied and duct-taped behind his back. He could only turn his head to look at his captors. They grabbed Jim by his arm, pulled him over the lip of the trunk, and rolled him out onto the ground with a thud.

Two Caucasian men dressed in khaki-colored security uniforms pulled Jim into a sitting position and leaned him against the bumper of the white Peugeot 206. A tall North African with sharp features walked up.

"Mr. Stillwater, it is you! I know you do not remember me, but I remember you *so* well. But more about that later. First, we must get you cleaned up. You will be my guest for just a few days, and we will make them as enjoyable as possible since they will be your last—unless you put on an exceptional performance. But more about that later too. Igor, help Mr. Stillwater to his cell, and please do not underestimate him. Boris, if Mr. Stillwater manages to grapple with Igor, shoot them both. Know that I will shoot you and Igor if Mr. Stillwater escapes and leaves either one of you alive," Johnathan said with a broad smile.

"Understood," Boris said as Igor nodded solemnly and began to help Jim to his feet.

Jim stumbled and noted that his visual field was narrowing; he was close to passing out as he stood up as straight as he could. Igor's huge hand wrapped almost all the way around Jim's arm below the bicep, and he led Jim toward what looked like three-sided concrete block dog kennels, painted white, with heavy-duty chain-link fencing and a gate enclosing each open side. A thatched roof provided shade.

"There is a water jug with ice in the corner and a shower attached to the wall if you want to cool off more. We will bring you dry clothes and a towel later," Igor said as he shoved Jim in and locked the gate with a padlock. Jim noticed a filthy old mattress on the concrete floor on the other side of the enclosure. It was all wet, apparently from recent use of the shower right across from it.

Jim rinsed out the plastic coffee mug attached to the ten-gallon water jug and noted that the water was both clear and cold. He filled the mug, hearing the ice shift inside the jug, and took a drink. Jim chugged down the first mug of water too quickly and was rewarded with a killer brain freeze. He poured another mug of water while allowing the headache to completely subside; he drank the second mug more slowly and then poured a third before he sat down on the wet mattress and started to take stock of his surroundings and opportunities for escape.

His thoughts were suddenly interrupted.

"Hey, asshole! Remember me?" a man yelled out with a heavy Russian accent as he approached the chain-link gate.

Jim turned his head slowly to see who was approaching, his face expressionless.

"I know that was you who took my gun! Too bad you won't be able to tell that tall bitch that I will hunt her down and kill her after we're done with you," the Russian from São Tomé boasted.

"Get away from him, you idiot. You heard what the boss said. Just open the gate so I can give him these clean clothes," Igor scolded as he walked up to the gate with a stack of neatly pressed street clothes and a couple of folded towels. "You stay where you are," he shouted at Jim, "and don't get up until I lock the gate again. Get dressed fast—you're having lunch with the boss."

Jim took another sip from his plastic mug and watched in mild amusement as the two Russians shoved each other and headed around the corner toward what appeared to be the main compound. He got up and picked up the stack of clothes, finding underwear, a T-shirt, khaki pants, and a checkered blue button-down shirt all neatly pressed and folded, sandwiched between two beach towels. He checked the sizes and noted that they were all his size.

Jim looked around out of modesty before he stripped off his rancid clothing and walked over to the outdoor shower along the wall. There was only one valve, and the water was barely lukewarm, which was welcome in the ninety-five-degree heat. Jim showered and felt reenergized after spending only a few minutes under the water, ignoring the fact that the drain seemed to be partially clogged and water was flowing across the concrete floor to soak the mattress even more.

The strong flow of water suddenly seemed to slow, and Jim guessed that the cistern feeding the shower was running low. He turned off the water, toweled himself off, and dressed, just now realizing that his hosts had not provided him shoes or socks. Jim pulled his wet boots back on, leaving his dirty, wet socks hanging on the fence to eventually dry in the humid air.

Not wanting to sit on the wet mattress and get his pants wet, Jim paced back and forth, examining the construction of his pen. "This really was a kennel at some point," he muttered under his breath.

In what seemed like an hour but was certainly less, Igor, Boris, and Dimitri, the Russian from São Tomé, strolled up to the gate and unlocked it. Boris and Dimitri carried Czech Scorpion machine pistols. Igor carried a three-foot-long cattle prod, and he seemed anxious to try it out on Jim.

"OK, Stillwater, come with us. You walk beside me without any trouble, and the boss will fill you in over lunch. Don't forget—if you escape, the boss will kill us all, so that's not happening. Anyhow, aren't you curious about what brought you here? The boss is a fucking genius, and with a little bit of Russian ingenuity, he is going to change Africa. You will see."

Jim stepped out of the kennel and walked beside Igor as the other two Russians covered them with their machine pistols. He noticed a classic Victorian home on top of a rise in the distance. Numerous corrugated-steel outbuildings and what looked like a

1950s two-story motel made the Victorian home seem very out of place.

As they walked closer to the house, Jim recognized the same African man who had greeted him earlier now sitting in a rocking chair and smoking a water pipe. The man smiled as the group approached, and when Jim was at the steps leading up to the front porch, the man took a long draw on his water pipe and then stood up.

"Welcome to my home away from home, courtesy of the previous colonial landlords," Johnathan said with a heartfelt laugh.

"So where do I know you from?" Jim asked.

"Oh, you do not know me, but I will never forget you," Johnathan replied sternly. He sat back down and took a long slow puff from the water pipe before speaking again. "Mr. Stillwater, you were standing outside my house watching triple S carry out a raid and take away my father from our family home when I was only fourteen years old. My father was never heard from or seen again."

"I'm sorry for your loss," Jim replied.

"Sorry? Triple S was doing your bidding. Do you not even remember him?" Johnathan spoke harshly.

"I am sorry, and I do not. I worked in Nigeria for a while and observed many police and security operations. None of them were done at my bidding. Was your father arrested for kidnapping? Based on what you do for a living, maybe they picked up the right man," Jim said sarcastically.

"Kidnapping is not my business. It is only a tool for what we are doing, and soon you will play an important role," Johnathan said before turning and banging on the window behind him with his knuckles.

Two young men emerged with high-end Sony video cameras.

"Try to keep the security detail out of the shoots so we will not need to do as much editing," Johnathan instructed them.

"So, I guess you plan to cut my head off on your front porch," Jim said, now only slightly sarcastic.

"No, Mr. Stillwater, your demise will be much more dramatic and appear to be accidental. You will get to take the full credit for something we have been planning for a long time. First, though, I promised you lunch. Please join me inside," Johnathan said pleasantly. He got up and led the way through the door from which the two cameramen had emerged. The cameramen were now spread apart and filming Jim and Johnathan from different angles.

Inside, a lavish spread of African and Middle Eastern food was arranged on the dining room table off to the right of the main entryway. Jim entered and looked for an opportunity to grab Johnathan, but he noticed a fleeting glimmer under the other man's robe, and as he looked closer while Johnathan was walking, he realized that his host was holding a double-edged dagger in his hand, mostly hidden under his traditional tribal robe.

Johnathan felt Jim getting closer; he turned, gave Jim a stern look, and then smiled. "Mr. Stillwater, join me at the table and enjoy the feast. I will tell you what we are celebrating in short order," the man said as he sat on one side of the table and motioned for Jim to take the seat beside him, at the head of the table.

When Jim was seated, Johnathan reached out and began to pile food onto his own plate.

"I highly recommend the falafel," Johnathan said as he spooned baba ghanoush onto his plate next to the falafel.

Jim filled his plate too. He understood that if he was able to escape, he would need the calories, and in his state of near dehydration, he needed to replenish salt too.

"Mr. Stillwater, do you know why you are here?"

"Because you kidnapped me," Jim said with a smart-assed smirk.

"No, I mean why are any Americans or English here in Nigeria? The answer is because you need to feed your empires. First with slaves, now with oil. If you had not needed slaves, you would not have come here in the first place, and if you did not need our oil, you would cut your aid to Nigeria and soon disappear."

"So you plan to build electric cars for us now," Jim said sarcastically.

"Do not toy with me, Mr. Stillwater—my patience has limits," Johnathan said as he pointed sharply at Igor, who was standing in the doorway of the dining room.

Igor stepped forward and jammed the cattle prod he was holding into Jim's back; Jim convulsed and fell to the floor.

"Help him back into his seat," Johnathan instructed.

Igor bent over to help Jim back into the chair, and as he did, Jim twisted the heavy cattle prod out of Igor's hand and swung it in an arc that connected with Igor's clavicle. There was a sickening crack, and Igor's shoulder was destroyed by the blow. He fell to his knees, screaming in pain. Jim saw the two guards with the machine pistols step forward, so he dropped the cattle prod and raised his hands in the air.

"Do not toy with me," Jim said in a low voice.

The guards looked at Johnathan for direction.

"Igor, take yourself to the infirmary. Mr. Stillwater, please return to your seat, or we will kill you now and proceed without your help."

Jim returned to his seat and watched Johnathan until he began eating again. Jim started eating too, waiting for the other man to return to his speech.

"As we were discussing, you are here because we have oil. If we do not have oil for you to steal, you will go away," Johnathan said before pausing for Jim to reply.

"And the kidnapping is intended to keep us from drilling for oil?" Jim asked skeptically.

"No, the kidnapping was intended to keep environmentalists, inspectors, and small competitors away. I did not start the kidnapping; I simply take advantage of the pattern. The former American general who advises the government could have easily eliminated the kidnapping using the Nigerian military, but instead, he has carefully targeted the kidnappings, and both he and the government continue to benefit from the ransoms and the environment that the publicity about the kidnappings creates."

"Interesting theory," Jim said seriously.

"Oh, it is not a theory," Johnathan said smugly.

"And now you'll replace the English and the Americans with Russians. I don't see how that will help you, other than satisfying your need for revenge."

"The Russians were somewhat accidental. The general brought them here for security and to use their spill-mitigation technology. As more security men returned home to Russia, the word spread about our movement. Russia saw the opportunity to destabilize Nigeria and eliminate some of the Nigerian oil from the market to force prices higher. When the oil is gone, they will leave too. You don't like it here very much, do you, Boris?" Johnathan ended in a louder voice as he turned his head toward Boris.

Boris ignored Johnathan's comment and continued to watch Jim closely.

"If you destroy the infrastructure, they will build it again. If you make the area hostile, they will just send more men to protect the oil rigs and move the refining to someplace else," Jim said with a slightly disgusted look on his face.

"Mr. Stillwater, you are correct. Fortunately, the world will believe that you have personally put a plan in place that will make the oil unrecoverable. I will show you how that will work tomorrow. Today, enjoy the food, and join me in the garden for drinks later this afternoon. We need to make sure that everyone is convinced that we are cooperating in this endeavor."

CHAPTER 16

MAIDUGURI, NIGERIA
16 1000 JULY

"Good morning, George! It is so good to see you," Colonel Ademe, the head of the SSS office in Maiduguri, greeted George. "Please introduce me to your two friends."

"Colonel, this is Hans Becker, retired colonel in the US Army, and this is Morgan Smith, a former special agent for the US government who now works as a consultant."

"Welcome to Maiduguri. Please sit down. Can I offer you coffee?"

"Yes, please," Morgan replied ahead of George and Hans as they all took a seat in front of the colonel's desk.

Colonel Ademe motioned to an orderly, and a silver tray with coffee service was brought in almost immediately and placed on a portable stand beside them. Colonel Ademe poured the steaming, aromatic black coffee.

"I understand that you're interested in the DIM?" Colonel Ademe asked politely.

"Yes, we think that they are involved in the kidnapping of an American. They had a price on his head and captured him during a ransom exchange for his wife," George answered.

"Did you gain the release of his wife, or do they still have her too?"

"They tried to keep her too, but we freed her," Morgan replied before she took a sip of the hot strong coffee.

"And her husband has a price on his head? That is quite unusual," the colonel said, apparently troubled.

"He worked in Nigeria when he was a young intelligence officer. His name is Jim Stillwater." George spoke up.

"Oh my God! Jim Stillwater? It must have been close to twenty years ago. I worked with him here, in Maiduguri, shortly after I was first assigned to triple S. I remember him well. He was providing training to us for raids and such. This all makes sense now! He was with us on the day that we captured Nelson Usama. DIM put a price on my head too for that day. Nelson was a communist, and we picked him up for interrogation, but he died of a heart attack en route to the police station. There were riots, and many people—especially his family—blamed us for killing him."

"Who put the price on your head? The communists?" Hans asked.

"Oh no, it was his son, Johnathan Usama, founder of the Dakar Islamist Mujahedeen, or DIM. That is the connection," Colonel Ademe explained.

"Do you keep track of them? Where can we start looking?" George asked impatiently.

"They have several properties in Maiduguri and probably fewer than fifty active members at their peak. They've been relatively quiet for the past year—some graffiti, a few firebombs thrown at police cars— but we haven't seen Johnathan for a few months and guessed that he was or is in another country receiving religious or military training. If he is paying for Jim, he may be here after all. We have plans in place with the army to raid their homes and businesses if they carry out a major attack. We can start hitting them as soon as tomorrow."

"Why wait?" Morgan asked.

"If we don't find him in the first place we raid, they'll just move him, and we will never catch up with them. If we wait until tomorrow, the army and mobile police can set roadblocks in place. We can also conduct several raids at the same time. So it is better to wait," the colonel said decisively.

"We understand, Colonel. Can we provide any assistance?" George asked.

"Maybe some drone coverage in the morning during the raids, in case they slip through our fingers, but we have what we need here to go after this small group. We believe that only a handful of them are armed, and it's unlikely that they will resist."

"My only worry is that they may decide to chop Jim's head off on camera without holding him in one place for too long," Hans said fearfully.

"I know how hard it is to sit and do nothing, and I expect that you three intend to do some digging as soon as you get out of here. I don't blame you, but how about this: Why don't you join us as we conduct some surveillance on our targets and meet with the army and police in preparation for our operations in the morning?"

"We will gladly accept your kind offer," George said as Hans and Morgan nodded in agreement.

"Excellent. We can take two cars as that won't attract as much attention. George, do you mind driving the second car? I'll drive the other car myself," the colonel said somewhat proudly. "But first, enjoy your coffee, and let me make a few calls." He smiled reassuringly.

After less than an hour, Colonel Ademe had things in place for the next morning and was ready to survey some of the raid and roadblock locations. "George, I expect that you are armed, but what about your friends?"

Morgan and Hans shook their heads.

"Very well. Come with me, and we will take care of that before we venture out," the colonel said before he led the way out of his office to the small-arms room down the hall. "We have some new Sig 9-millimeter pistols, thanks to your recent military aid. Will they be suitable, or would you prefer revolvers?" he asked.

"A Sig would be fine. Thank you," Morgan said.

"Sig for me too," Hans nodded.

The armorer issued the pistols and one spare magazine of ammunition. Morgan and Hans signed for them and tucked the pistols under their shirts.

"Very good. Now let us proceed," the colonel said before he led the group through the back door and into a fenced parking area. "George, you take the white 208, and I will take the other white 208," he joked as they looked at a row of at least a dozen white Peugeot 208 sedans. "Just pick one; the keys are in the ignition."

Colonel Ademe and Hans got into the closest car in the row, and George and Morgan climbed into the one beside it. An armed guard rolled back a covered gate, and the colonel led the way out of the lot and onto the highway that led to the center of town. It was close to noon, and traffic was heavy as many headed to the market or elsewhere for lunch. The air conditioners struggled to keep the interiors of the cars cool in the blistering heat, and Morgan guessed that the dark windows had been installed as much for comfort as security.

After about twenty minutes, Colonel Ademe pulled up in front of an Indian restaurant in a crowded neighborhood that was part commercial and part residential. He got out and motioned for George to park next to him. "It's time for lunch. Please join me inside," the colonel said as he led the way, walking past the hostess like she didn't exist and going straight to a table in the unoccupied corner by the front window.

The hostess hurried over to the table with menus in hand, placed them on the table, and disappeared into the back.

"Colonel, we can skip the lunch or make it quick; that would be OK by us," Hans suggested.

"This is one of the stops we need to make. You will see." Colonel Ademe smiled.

A tall Indian man emerged from the kitchen and hurried over to the table. He looked straight at the colonel and ignored the others. "The usual variety will be brought right out. How can I help you today, Colonel?" the man said with a slight stutter.

"Have you seen Johnathan or any of his friends in here in the past couple of weeks?" Colonel Ademe asked him politely.

"No, I absolutely have not. I have not seen any of them for several months," the Indian man added.

"If you do see any of them today or tomorrow, you call me directly. You know how to reach me," the colonel said, directing a stern gaze into the Indian man's eyes.

"Yes, Colonel. I understand. Your food will be right out. Beer too?"

The colonel nodded, and the man hurried away. In minutes another, smaller Indian with arms full of dishes hurried over to the table, and the hostess who had attempted to greet them rushed over with four large bottles of Nigerian beer.

"I recommend the tandoori chicken, but try a little of everything. And don't worry about taking the last bit of something; they will bring more," the colonel said with a smile.

"Has he worked for you very long?" Morgan asked.

"Only as long as he has owned the restaurant and needed the proper permits—three or four years. This is a popular place for dinner, and Johnathan lived in this neighborhood as a child and often comes back here to visit his friends. I thought that we might have gotten lucky, if he is staying nearby with some of them. We will go to a warehouse that his family owns on the other side of town after we finish our food."

After almost an hour of eating and a second round of beer, Colonel Ademe decided that it was time to go. "Lunchtime is over, so the traffic will have died down. It was better to sit with food and drink than sit in our cars. I will take us past the warehouse, and we will look for signs of activity as we pass by. There are never more than one or two cars there. A blue van that is broken down and never moves is parked by the loading dock. We cannot stop."

"We will keep you in sight, Colonel," George responded.

Colonel Ademe led the way across the city. Navigating many of the roads was difficult due to the roadside flea markets that stretched for miles. Pedestrians with heavy loads of goods carried on top of their heads walked, seemingly oblivious to the traffic, between the moving cars. In other places, the two-lane roads were limited to one lane for twenty meters at a time where cassava had been shredded and laid on top of the asphalt to dry.

As they neared the warehouse district, the crowds thinned, and so did the traffic. Container trucks with steel shipping containers sped down the middle of the narrow two-lane roads, and both the colonel and George were forced to drive along the shoulder three times in less than two blocks to avoid collisions.

Colonel Ademe finally swerved right and went down a side street, and George had time enough to turn since he was still hanging back to avoid the appearance of a convoy. Morgan saw the blue van sitting on flat tires behind the loading dock of the warehouse off to their right. "That must be the place!" she exclaimed.

"There are several cars parked outside—and a truck with a boat trailer," George commented.

"That boat is the same kind that they were using for the prisoner exchange. Jim might be in there right now. We can't wait until morning," Morgan said excitedly.

"We'll talk to the colonel in a couple of minutes. He's stopping at the army barracks about three miles up the road. I don't have a signal here, so I can't call him," George replied as he sped up and closed some of the distance between their cars.

At the army barracks, Colonel Ademe showed his credentials to two soldiers with rifles manning the gate, and the brightly painted barrier was raised, allowing both cars entry. The cars pulled into empty spaces in front of the building. As they all emerged from the cars, Morgan yelled over to the colonel, "That boat on the trailer was the same kind that they used in the ransom exchange!"

"I saw the boat and suspected as much. This is the first time we have observed a boat at that location, and there is little need for a boat in Maiduguri," Colonel Ademe said solemnly.

"Can we hit the place before morning?" George asked hopefully.

"We will discuss that with the army officers inside and see whether they can spare enough of their soldiers to isolate the warehouse before we conduct a raid. Now let's go in."

CHAPTER 17

RAMSTEIN AFB, KAISERSLAUTERN, GERMANY
16 1500 JULY

"Good afternoon, ladies. I hope that your leisurely morning schedule and lunch in Kaiserslautern were enjoyable. The doctor mentioned to me this morning that you were prescribed Primaquine for the malaria, but fortunately, you have no other health concerns." Special Agent Rob Duncan greeted Gwen and Tanya in the reception area of the small FBI office on the sprawling US Air Force base located on the outskirts of Kaiserslautern, Germany.

"We are both feeling much better. Is there any word on Jim?" Gwen got right to the point.

"No, I'm afraid not, but I spoke with the DEA's local attaché this morning, and he was headed to Maiduguri with Hans and Morgan. The DEA have some connections with law enforcement there," Rob answered.

"I spoke with Morgan this morning before she got on the plane to Maiduguri. She promised to call with any updates,"

Tanya said as she stepped into the conference room and flopped down in one of the high-backed leather chairs that lined the table.

A US Army Special Forces master sergeant who was seated at the table didn't say a word as Tanya and then Gwen entered the room and took a seat.

"I think I remember Jim mentioning that he spent time in Maiduguri while he was working in Nigeria years ago," Gwen said with a creased brow.

"You're right. I have his military record right here," the master sergeant spoke for the first time.

"Gwen, Tanya, this is Master Sergeant Hemminger," Rob said as he sat down next to the burly soldier.

"Pleased to meet you," the master sergeant said. After standing to shake hands with both Gwen and Tanya, he resumed his seat.

"I really appreciate your willingness to spend some time with me today. We have a few more angles that we would like to attack. We have not had any luck identifying any members of the local Biafra independence movement, so I thought that we would try something else. We have some intel that Boko Haram is trying to make inroads in the south and may even want to gain revenue from smuggled oil the way ISIL did in Iraq. I have some photos of the BH members who have been seen in the south lately, so you let me know if any of them look familiar, OK?" Rob said before he used a remote to turn on the projection screen at the front of the room.

Gwen watched over Rob's shoulder as he navigated through folders on the FBI laptop that was plugged into a projector cable through the hole in the center of the table.

"Before we get started, is there anything else that you have thought of that might be important? Even some small detail that seems unimportant could help us find Jim," Rob said in an encouraging tone.

"There is one thing..." Gwen responded hesitantly. "When we were scuba diving just before we were captured, Tanya and I were surveying some oil damage on the reef. The oil looked brown, like it had detergent or an emulsifying agent mixed in with it. I got some of the brown goo on my sleeve, which made an impression on me because it was a brand-new Lycra stinger suit, and I knew that the oil would stain it. The funny thing is, after two days, the blotch of oil on my sleeve was completely gone, and the fabric was bleached completely white. I thought at first that our captors had bleached it when they washed some of our clothes, but it turns out that they never washed the stinger suit. It still smells like seaweed, since it was never even rinsed out."

"The same thing happened with an oil stain on my thigh. It looks like someone spilled Clorox on the stinger suit," Tanya added.

"Why do you think that might be important?" Rob inquired, somewhat puzzled.

"I think they kidnapped us to hide the fact that they spilled oil in São Tomé during their exploratory oil drilling," Gwen said accusingly.

Rob looked a bit skeptical, and Master Sergeant Hemminger rolled his eyes but remained silent.

Tanya noted their reactions and decided to jump in. "This might be an even bigger deal than it seems. I spoke to Morgan about their dive when she, Jim, and Hans were still looking for clues in São Tomé. They went to the same dive site, and they're certain that they were in the right place, since they found the anchor that our captain had cut loose and left behind when he ran away from our captors. That whole area was completely bleached for as far as Jim and Morgan could see. Bleaching is a big problem all around the world right now, but it normally takes months or even years to destroy that much coral. This happened in one week, and oh, by the way, they didn't see a drop of oil or brown goo."

"So, you think that the pirates are using something to get rid of the oil spills that is also causing coral bleaching—and they kidnapped you to cover it up?" Rob asked, still skeptical.

As Rob spoke, Master Sergeant Hemminger dug through a stack of folders in front of him and leafed through one displaying classification warnings and code words that Tanya did not recognize. When Rob had finished speaking, the master sergeant tossed a couple of photos in front of him.

"Those photos were taken by an informant who was working as part of a security team that O'Finn sent to Nigeria. Those barrels in the background in the first photo were offloaded from a Russian ship at Port Harcourt. In the second photo, you can see a barge fitted with spray equipment that we originally thought was for fire suppression, but we have seen them reload these barges with fifty barrels at a time and never saw any fires anywhere near where they were operating," Master Sergeant Hemminger said, snatching the photos back from Rob before he could pass them to Tanya and Gwen.

"I will need copies of those, Sergeant," Rob said in a stronger tone than he had used previously in the presence of Gwen and Tanya.

"There were barrels like that at the camp where we were held. And they had Cyrillic biohazard markings on them," Tanya said.

"Thousands of them, and they kept them under heavy guard," Gwen added.

Master Sergeant Hemminger looked concerned for the first time and handed another folder to Rob. "We think that the Russians experimented with a biohazardous agent meant for oil-spill mitigation. For some reason, they discontinued its use and went back to the conventional detergents after a few test runs in the Caspian Sea. One of the big Western oil companies used something similar after a gigantic spill in the Gulf of Mexico. A lot of environmentalists claimed that all it did was make the oil sink to the bottom, where it continued to kill marine life. We don't have any evidence of that, though," the master sergeant ended introspectively.

"I'll pass this along to headquarters," Rob said to him quietly.

"Time for some pictures?" Tanya asked impatiently.

"Yes, we'll get started," Rob answered as he opened a folder on his laptop and started to show a collection of mug shots and candid photos of Boko Haram members.

Gwen and Tanya paid close attention and asked Rob to back up a few times, but after more than an hour, they had not recognized any of the faces. Rob now seemed frustrated and was going through another set of folders on his laptop while Gwen continued to peek at what he was doing.

"Wait! Go back to that folder," Gwen exclaimed.

Rob was irritated that Gwen had been watching the screen over his shoulder but complied and showed her the previous photo.

"Holy shit! That's him!" Tanya screamed as she saw the now familiar face appear on the screen.

"That's their leader. Who is he?" Gwen asked.

"That is Johnathan Usama, founder of the Dakar Islamic Mujahedeen and the man who we believe put the bounty out on your husband," Rob replied, more than a little shocked.

"He is *not* in Maiduguri; he's somewhere near Port Harcourt, in the delta," Tanya yelled.

"Oh fuck," Master Sergeant Hemminger exclaimed, before looking embarrassed at swearing in front of women.

"I've gotta call Morgan," Tanya said as she pulled out her phone and repeatedly hit the redial without success.

"I'll call the DEA," Rob said, excusing himself before hurrying to his office down the hall.

"We need to call Jorge! He and his boys are watching Mosby at Eclectic Manor," Gwen blurted out.

"Why call now?" Tanya asked, completely exasperated.

"Jorge's boys, Patrick and Miles, are computer geniuses. I'll bet that they can use the Internet to find oil rigs stuck up in the mangroves around Port Harcourt. They've been playing around with machine learning techniques since they were in elementary school. Oil rigs are big, and they don't belong in the middle of some pirate or terrorist camp. They've got to be able to do this!" Gwen exclaimed decisively.

CHAPTER 18

MAIDUGURI, NIGERIA
16 1600 JULY

George, Morgan, and Hans sat in the dayroom at the army base, impatiently waiting for Colonel Ademe to return from his meeting with the Nigerian army.

"The cell service here sucks," Morgan complained.

"You can't use your cell phone in here. They have jammers to keep Boko Haram from targeting the base with mortar fire. They're pretty sure that someone inside the base was adjusting fire last year when they were attacked," George explained.

"Wow, that sucks even more. We might get attacked, and we can't even call for help," Morgan kidded.

"How soon does it get dark this time of year?" Hans asked suddenly and rather seriously.

"I think sometime between seven and eight. And I get your point—we don't have a lot of time left, unless these guys want to do things in the dark. If they don't have night vision devices for everyone like we do in the US SOF, they'll want to operate in daylight so that they don't shoot at one another," George answered.

"Good plan," Morgan said as she got up and paced. She was just turning near the door when Colonel Ademe opened it and hurried into the room.

"I am so sorry for taking so long. We were attempting to get floor plans for the warehouse, but the best we could do was speak with a fire inspector who was in the building last year. He said that it's mostly empty except for a row of offices along the north wall on the second floor. There are stairs at either end, and a freight elevator in the northwest corner that wasn't working when he conducted his inspection," the colonel explained.

"Are we going to do this today?" Morgan pressed.

"Yes, the military is already departing the barracks and will have the warehouse secured and cleared within the hour. We need to remain here until that time. My one concern is that the general in charge insisted on calling the fire department to have them check on the status of the building, and we know nothing about that man's allegiances, so he could have warned any occupants that the Nigerian army was inquiring about the warehouse."

"So I guess we wait," George said, sitting back down.

"Fortunately, the warehouse is close by," Hans said as he sat back down too.

After less than forty-five minutes, a tall, slender Nigerian army corporal sauntered into the room and approached Colonel Ademe.

"Sir, General Butoma sent me to tell you that they have secured the building as you requested. There were no occupants, but it looks like someone has been there within the past couple of days. The general will greet you when you arrive."

"OK, let's go," George said as he jumped to his feet.

The four of them hurried outside and piled into their vehicles, and even the colonel seemed to be in a hurry. "I have never seen him move so fast," Morgan said to George when they were inside their car.

"He knows that there will not be much of a crime scene left once the army is done with the place, and the longer we take to get there, the more stuff will be pilfered by the soldiers. They're not paid much here," George explained.

"It's not all that different from even Western armies. I was an enlisted MP in the US Army before I became a fed," Morgan replied.

In less than ten minutes, they arrived at the warehouse and immediately noticed the soldiers guarding the perimeter fence line. There were two armored cars with their guns still pointed at the building, a couple of stake-bed trucks used to transport the infantry, and a Mercedes sedan with little flags mounted above its headlights, indicating that it was the general's car.

Colonel Ademe pulled his Peugeot up next to the Mercedes, and George pulled in behind him.

"George, you three go inside and look around. I will speak with the general," the colonel waved his hand as if to send the three Americans away.

"You know what that's about," Hans said to George as they headed across the nearly empty warehouse parking lot.

"Yeah, the general will expect a favor from the colonel since he and his men went to all of this effort and didn't come up with a single thing that the general could brag about to his superiors."

"Those armored cars are not cheap to drive around in either. They get about three miles per gallon," Morgan added.

"At least fuel is cheap here." Hans chortled.

When they got inside the warehouse, soldiers were still milling about, and George pointed out that several of the soldiers had removed the fire axes and extinguishers from the walls and were carrying them out to the trucks in the parking lot.

"Spoils of war," Hans said knowingly.

"Not much to look through now; they've stolen everything that wasn't nailed down," Morgan said with a frown. "Hey, we'd better check out that boat outside before they take that too," she added.

"You and Hans check out the boat. I'll head upstairs and see if I can find anything in the offices," George said before he hurried toward the stairs.

When Morgan and Hans stepped back outside, General Butoma was waving his arms for his men to depart, and Colonel Ademe was walking toward them.

"George went upstairs. We're going to check out the boat," Morgan yelled across the parking lot over the noise of the military vehicles starting up their engines.

The colonel waved in acknowledgment and headed inside the warehouse.

"I guess the army doesn't need a boat." Hans laughed.

"We're in the fuckin' desert," Morgan replied with a grin as she climbed up on the boat trailer and looked inside the sixteen-foot fiberglass boat.

"Check out the machine gun mounts on both sides. I don't think that they plan to use this for fishing," Hans said.

"No kidding. I found some empty brass that rolled back into the stern. Seven six two by fifty-four," Morgan said as she picked up one of the expended rounds and held it up to her nose. "This was fired in the past couple of days. Probably from a PKM. It might have even been fired at us," she added as she stuffed the round into her pocket to show George later.

"Not much here. Let's see if George came up with anything," Hans suggested.

Morgan agreed, and both she and Hans headed back into the warehouse, where George was waiting for them by the freight elevator.

"Morgan, take a look inside the elevator and tell me if you see anything special," George said with a smile.

Morgan ducked under the bright-orange engineer tape across the open door of the freight elevator, stepped in, and then quickly stepped back out and closer to George. "There's a *B* button. This place has a basement," she said in a very low voice.

"It sure does, and there is almost always another way into a basement besides the elevator," George answered in a very low voice as the colonel joined their huddle.

"This place is built on a slab, and the only break in it that I can see is where this elevator shaft was formed when they poured the slab," Hans said.

Both George and Colonel Ademe looked surprised.

"He's an engineer," Morgan clarified with a smile.

"My guess is that there's a covered shaft with either a ladder or stairs just outside the building—probably by the loading dock for convenience," Hans continued.

"The army did not find the basement. The general told me that they cleared the first floor and the upstairs. I'm glad that I gave you those weapons. The problem is that the army cut the power to the building, so there won't be any lights downstairs, but I do have flashlights in the trunks of both cars," Colonel Ademe added.

"What are we waiting for?" Morgan asked as she headed toward the loading dock.

"The last of the army vehicles are just leaving. Should we stop them?" Hans asked.

"No way in hell," George said as he watched the last armored car drive away. At almost the same second, his cell phone and Morgan's started to ring.

Morgan and George answered their phones.

"The guy who put the bounty out on Jim is not in Maiduguri; he's in the south and was in charge of the camp where Gwen and Tanya were held," Morgan shouted and waved excitedly at George.

"That's what the FBI is telling me right now," George shouted back and returned to his call.

"As soon as we check this place out, we need to get down to Port Harcourt," Morgan announced.

"Why do we still need to check this place out?" Colonel Ademe asked.

"The warehouse is still connected somehow. Hans and I found machine gun mounts and fresh brass on the boat," Morgan said as she pulled the 7.62x54 Russian shell out of her pocket and handed it to the colonel, who nodded, seemingly convinced.

Hans walked over to them from the loading dock. "I found the way in, and it has a big ass padlock on it, so nobody is in there unless they're being held prisoner. They took all the fire axes, so there is only one way I know of to take care of that lock," Hans said to the colonel.

"Go ahead and shoot it off. I'll get the flashlights," the colonel said as he ran to his car and hurried back with two police flashlights.

Hans made quick work of the lock and pulled open the heavy steel hatch. Stairs descended under the building. Everyone had their weapons out and ready.

"If there is anyone down there, they know we're coming," George said softly as he picked up a fist-sized piece of concrete. "Come out with your hands up, or we will throw in a grenade!" George yelled.

They waited about thirty seconds, but nobody answered.

"OK, here comes the first grenade," George said as he tossed the piece of concrete down the stairs, where it hit the bottom with a thud.

"No, wait!" someone shouted from down below.

"Come up the stairs with your hands up!" George ordered.

As George and Colonel Ademe pointed their weapons down the stairs and shone the flashlights into the dark basement, an African man in his thirties emerged into the sunlight and walked hesitantly up the stairs.

"Triple S. Keep your hands up, or I will shoot you," the colonel warned.

The man complied and stepped up onto the pavement of the parking lot.

"Now get on your knees," the colonel ordered.

The man complied once again and started to sob as George moved forward, shoved the man face-first onto the asphalt, and searched him while Colonel Ademe kept him covered.

182

"He's clean. Here's his wallet," George said and tossed it to the colonel.

"Is there anyone else down there?" Colonel Ademe demanded.

"No, just me," the man sobbed.

"Where is the American?" Morgan demanded.

"What American?"

"The hostage!" Morgan elaborated.

"All of the hostages are in the south. I don't know where exactly. I just bring things up here for them," the man answered earnestly.

"You are coming with us when we go down there, and if there is anyone else down there, you will be the first one I shoot," Colonel Ademe warned.

"There is nobody," the man sniffled.

The colonel grabbed the man by the arm and pushed him along in front of him as they descended the stairs. George hung back a little but followed them down, and both Morgan and Hans headed down too, Morgan using her cell phone for additional light.

"Weapons racks full of AKM assault rifles, PKM machine guns, RPG-7 V grenade launchers, and a money-counting cage," George said in disbelief as he looked around.

"I work in there," the man offered, pointing to the money-counting machines and the stacks of dollars, euros, and naira.

"Money and guns," Hans whistled admiringly.

"All we need are some lawyers," Morgan joked.

"I am a lawyer," the African man said seriously, not understanding the musical reference.

"How did you get down here? Did they lock you in?" George asked him.

"I used the elevator. It is not really broken; we just disable it at the breaker box most of the time and put up an Out of Order sign. But when the power went out, I could not leave," the man responded, a smile spreading across his face.

"How much money is down here?" Morgan asked.

"Approximately seven million US dollars in mixed currencies," the man said very proudly.

"From kidnapping people," Hans said sharply.

"Yes, I am afraid you are correct, but I just count the money and move it into banks," the man said defensively.

"I need to call the base, and hopefully some of the officers will still be there," Colonel Ademe said before he walked up the stairs and out of the basement.

"That general is going to shit his pants when he finds out what he left on the table," Hans laughed gleefully.

"OK, but we need to get going," Morgan urged.

"There aren't any planes to Port Harcourt until morning," George said as he looked through the racks of weapons. "I'll call the office and have someone get us on the first flight out."

"I have some soldiers on the way," Colonel Ademe interjected, "so I suggest that we close this place up and park a car in front of the entrance. We can't do much else until the power is turned back on at the pole. I heard you say that you're heading to Port Harcourt. I'll notify the triple S office that you're coming. Colonel Bete is in charge there. Do you know him, George?"

"Yes, the DEA have done some work with his office, and he's visited me in Abuja."

"Very good. We will squeeze this one a bit and see what he can tell us that might help you," Colonel Ademe said before he grabbed their prisoner, handcuffed him with the handcuffs he had retrieved from his car, and pushed him back up the stairs, the others following close behind. "Tonight will be a long night, and we will still be conducting the series of raids. That's even more important after seeing the kind of resources that these criminals have amassed. The motor park at my office will be closed, but the duty sergeant and an armorer will be on duty, so just park out front and turn in your weapons and car keys before you take your own car back to the hotel."

"We aren't leaving you here by yourself with a prisoner and all that stuff. We can wait until your men get here," George said as he patted the colonel on the shoulder.

"Thank you, George. This has turned into a very interesting day. I hope that tomorrow you will find out where Mr. Stillwater is being held. Please ask him whether he remembers me," Colonel Ademe replied with a fond smile.

CHAPTER 19

DELTA STATE, NIGERIA
17 0700 JULY

Jim had chosen to sleep between the two beach towels on a dry spot on the concrete floor instead of on the waterlogged mattress. He had leaned the mattress vertically against the wall in the hope that it would dry out in case he needed to spend another night in the kennel. He dozed off for a few minutes at a time and was wakened frequently by both mosquitoes and the hard surface he was sleeping on. The call to prayer had just finished, and he was trying to get a bit more sleep when he heard the lock being opened. Another stack of dry clothes and towels was deposited on the floor before the gate was slammed shut.

"We will be back in half an hour. Get dressed so that you look nice for the camera," an unfamiliar Russian voice announced loudly. "Do you hear me?"

"Yes, thirty minutes, and I'm awake," Jim said groggily as he sat up.

Jim went over and examined the stack of clothing and towels. Just like yesterday, there were khaki slacks, a button-down shirt, a

T-shirt, and underwear, but today, a pair of socks and a comb had been added to the mix. After taking a quick shower, he toweled off and dressed, and by the time he was ready, three other Russians had shown up to escort him out.

"You're going to the mess hall for breakfast. You may not get much for lunch, since we're headed out for the day to see the *ochistitel*," a heavy older man with a KGB border guard tattoo on his arm said in Russian.

"What's that?" Jim asked.

"You'll see. Now move. This cattle prod might not be as big, but it hurts just as much," the Russian said, holding up a handheld device.

"If you don't use it on me, I won't use it on you," Jim proposed with an agreeable smile.

"You are a very funny guy—especially for someone in your position," the Russian replied with a grin. "The other two don't know English very well, so be careful what you do, or they will shoot you without warning," he cautioned.

Jim noted that the two guards were again armed with Scorpion submachine pistols.

They arrived at the mess hall after a ten-minute walk. Jim was led to the head table and told to sit down. The two cameramen were already filming when Johnathan came in, sat down next to Jim, and motioned for the food to be served.

"Good morning, Mr. Stillwater. I trust that you had a fairly miserable night," Johnathan said with a big smile. "I just wanted to pass along that the man whose shoulder you broke is no longer experiencing any pain. It was going to be complicated to provide him medical care without taking him into Port Harcourt, so we shot him and the two men he had handpicked to assist him. I assure you that the men guarding you today are aware of what happened."

"How kind of you," Jim replied levelly.

"Today we will film you inspecting the *inhenishta*—or *ochistitel*, as the Russians call it—that we have been saving up for a rainy day. That rainy day will be tomorrow. We now have enough of the cleaner so that when we inject it into the wells distributed across the offshore oil field, it will become biologically self-sustaining. It will literally digest one of the largest oil reservoirs in the world. Within months, the oil field will be abandoned, and we will establish a caliphate free from foreign interference. People here will live as they did before the oil was found," Johnathan said with immense pride.

"You mean that you'll lead your people back into the Stone Age. And I expect you plan to treat your people with medical needs the same way you treated the Russians," Jim replied, utterly disgusted.

"The best part of this story is that the Americans will be blamed for yet another racist plot. It will be clear that you tricked us into injecting the *inhenishta* into the wells, and we will put you on trial in our Islamic court and execute you for the world to see. If you cooperate, that is how it will happen. But who knows? If you stay alive for a couple more days, you might be rescued. If you do not agree to cooperate, I will kill you now and simply claim that we caught you performing your mischief. Your previous connections to the American intelligence community will be enough to support the conspiracy theories that the Russians will spread across news groups and blogs."

"It sounds like you've been planning all of this for a while," Jim said.

"More than three years. Now, do you agree to my terms?" Johnathan pressed.

"OK," Jim answered reluctantly.

"Then shake my hand. I don't know why, but I am told that it means something to you," Johnathan said as he held out his hand.

Jim shook it.

"Now, let us eat. We have a busy day ahead," Johnathan said with a broad smile.

After thirty minutes of eating breakfast, Johnathan led Jim out the back of the mess hall. Jim saw the same acres of barrels behind security fencing that Tanya and Gwen had noticed before. This morning the gates were unlocked, and security guards were posted around the perimeter. Forklifts were moving back and forth, loading barrels onto trucks, as Johnathan guided Jim through the maze of activity and inspected the progress of his workers. The cameramen continued to film, and Johnathan, who was very aware of the cameras, would smile directly at them while he placed a hand on Jim's shoulder.

After almost an hour of this, Johnathan led Jim to two Toyota Land Rovers. Jim was instructed to get into one of the vehicles with the three Russian guards; Johnathan and the two cameramen got into the vehicle in front of it, and they all headed out of the compound on a one-lane gravel causeway with mangrove swamps on both sides.

Jim looked around as much as possible without being too obvious about it. He was surprised that his captors had not blindfolded him for when the cameras weren't rolling, and he didn't want to give them a reason to do so now.

"Hey, Stillwater, just take it easy, and we'll take you out of here with us. Johnathan is fucking crazy, but he doesn't want to kill you until he blows up one of the oil rigs after injecting the wells."

"Let's get out of here now. I'll make sure that you don't face any criminal charges," Jim suggested.

"Good idea, but no, we can't do that. We need to make sure that the *ochistitel* gets injected into the wells. If we fail at that after all of this effort, our own government will kill us," the Russian reasoned.

"Why would they do that? I thought that Russia wanted to control the oil fields in West Africa the same way that China is securing the oil on the east coast?" Jim asked with a creased brow.

"Stillwater, Russia doesn't need more oil; Russia needs to control production to keep the price up. Our infrastructure is old and inefficient, and it costs us more to extract the oil that we have at home. OPEC doesn't have the power to cut oil production to jack up the price, and Nigeria won't cut production because they need the oil revenue. Are you starting to figure this shit out, Stillwater? The only possible play is to take a large amount of the oil off the market permanently. All we had to do was convince Johnathan that it would help him establish a caliphate, and that part wasn't very hard to do."

"So how does O'Finn fit into this?" Jim asked skeptically.

"I don't know who that is."

"An American general who's working for the Nigerians," Jim prompted.

"Nah, not ringing a bell. Now, do we have an agreement? You don't try to escape, and we take you out of here with us when shit hits the fan."

"What's your name?" Jim asked.

"I am Ivan," the man responded with a smile and held out his hand to shake.

"Oh, that's believable!" Jim scoffed.

"Hey, don't make fun. Stereotypes start someplace, right?" Ivan replied openly.

"All right," Jim said as he quickly shook Ivan's hand.

Jim didn't trust the Russian and suspected that Ivan was just using a ploy to keep him from attempting to escape and thus getting him killed as the other Russian guards had been killed. He decided to play along in case his other options ran out and on the small chance that Ivan was telling the truth.

"OK, Stillwater, we're here. Smile for the camera," Ivan teased as the Rover emerged from the mangroves into an open area. There were docks and a rusted oil rig beached in the mud on the other side of an estuary that led to the ocean.

Johnathan got out of the other Rover, sauntered up to Jim, and put his arm around Jim's shoulder as the two cameramen filmed them.

"Stillwater, I trust you had a pleasant ride? I suspect that the Russians were not very good company; their sense of humor is very different, and these three seem so serious all of the time. No matter, this will be an interesting morning. First, we will inspect the barges. We have six barges, and each one is loaded with twenty barrels of the *inhenista* and connected to a high-pressure pump. Can you believe it? We didn't even need to make these, since the oil company designed them to spray oil slicks when they spilled oil. All we needed to do was modify the nozzle so that it clamps onto the well and cuts a hole in it to inject the *inhenista*. Our Russian friends did that part for us," Johnathan bragged.

"They gave you the *inhenista* too," Jim guessed.

"Oh my, no. That is the hilarious part. The American general who is working for the government bought the *inhenista* and smuggled it here. He has no idea how much he has helped us, despite his speeches about stopping piracy and terrorism in Nigeria."

"Ironic," Jim commented wryly.

"Greed, Mr. Stillwater. It is always easy to manipulate greedy men." Johnathan smiled and started to stroll forward to the docks.

"Greed for power is no different than greed for money," Jim answered as he walked beside Johnathan.

"If you meant that as yet another attempt to provoke me, then you do not understand me. All power belongs to Allah," Johnathan said as an African workman with a clipboard ran up to greet him.

"Emir, all of the *inhenista* is loaded, and the pumps were all tested yesterday," the workman said proudly.

"Very good. Tomorrow we will change the world, inshalla," Johnathan replied.

"Emir, the security team is ready to demonstrate taking over the rig," the workman stated, gesturing toward the oil rig on the other side of the estuary.

Johnathan pulled out his phone and sent a text. Moments later, four speedboats revved their engines and raced across the estuary toward the oil rig. One of the boats orbited around the rig, firing a machine gun at the deck of the rig while the other three boats were tied off to the legs of the rig and armed men started up the ladders. Jim noticed that as these men were ascending, other men in the boats were attaching satchel charges to the legs of the rig.

One of the barges was underway toward the rig. The attackers were now in full control of the rig, and the small-arms fire ceased. The barge maneuvered to the well pipe in the center, and Jim watched as the nozzle on the end of a hydraulic arm was mated with the pipe and clamped in place. Black diesel smoke poured out of the barge as the high-pressure pumps were turned on. The captain blew the barge's foghorn three times to indicate that the *inhenista* was flowing into the well.

The attackers on top of the rig threw lines out and rapidly rappelled down to the speedboats that they had emerged from. The three boats departed, and the fourth boat that had been orbiting the rig moved in and picked up the crew from the barge. Once all four boats were clear of the barge, the satchel charges were detonated, apparently remotely, and the rig collapsed as if in slow motion.

Johnathan clapped his hands in applause. "Mr. Stillwater, tomorrow morning, this will be repeated simultaneously at six locations calculated to do the most damage to the Nigerian oil fields. You will be on board one of the barges, but I do not know whether you will be extracted in time to avoid some obviously severe damage."

"Impressive," Jim commented.

CHAPTER 20

PORT HARCOURT, NIGERIA
17 1300 JULY

George, Hans, and Morgan arrived in Port Harcourt on the first flight of the day from Maiduguri. The midday heat was overpowering when the door of the 727 opened and the three descended the stairs onto the tarmac. They headed straight for the airport gate door, and although they were counting on air-conditioned relief from the blast of heat, they were greeted instead by damp, stagnant air as they walked through a tunnel, awkwardly dragging their wheelie suitcases behind them.

Two SSS agents were waiting for the three travelers at the security checkpoint. "Agent West?" one of them stepped forward and addressed George.

"Yes," George responded as the SSS agent showed his credentials and George reciprocated.

"My name is Major Entebe. Colonel Bete sends his regards. Colonel Ademe called me this morning and explained the situation. He also asked me to thank you once more for your help with the takedown yesterday. They finished the inventory just a few hours ago. Are these your associates?" the major asked, pointing at Hans and Morgan.

"Yes, they were with me and Colonel Ademe yesterday for the takedown," George said.

"Welcome to Port Harcourt. You can drop your bags off at my office here at the airport before we head to our plane. I am afraid that airplanes and boats are the only options we have to help us monitor many of our coastal villages. That is why piracy has flourished in this area. Now please follow me," Major Entebe said as he led the three Americans around the security checkpoint and into a back area of the airport not open to the public.

The hallways were narrow and dirty, but this part of the airport was air-conditioned, fortunately. The sudden cold air hitting their sweat-soaked clothing made Hans and Morgan shiver, and they exchanged meaningful smiles as they squeezed into the agent's small office. One wall was lined with CCTV monitors while the other was covered with plaques and family photos of the major and a very large family.

"Are those your children?" Morgan asked Major Entebe as she stepped over to the wall for a closer look.

"Why yes, all six of them, and that is my wife in the middle," he answered proudly.

"They look like a wonderful family," Morgan complimented him.

"Yes, but sometimes they can be a handful for my wife, especially when I was younger and working all over Nigeria."

"That seems to be one of the things that all military and law enforcement members have in common," George added.

"Well, hopefully you'll get home on time tonight," Hans put in.

"Yes, hopefully so. I understand that we are looking for some facilities that are quite large—a camp with many boats, supplies, and even an old oil rig. That means that it is very close to the coast, so maybe we will find them quickly," Major Entebe said optimistically.

"Yes, hopefully so," George agreed.

"Please place your bags over there against the wall. They will be kept safe. I have maps for you here. Would you like me to bring an extra camera for the airplane ride?" the major asked.

"That would be great," Morgan said as she stepped forward to accept a camera bag and one of the maps from the major, leaving her own luggage to lean against the wall beside the men's two suitcases.

"All right, let's go," Major Entebe said as he waved them out of the office. He pulled the door closed behind him and then paused to lock the deadbolt on the door.

The major led them down the filthy and dimly lit hallway toward an exit sign at the end. When he pushed the crash bar on the door and they burst out onto the airport tarmac, the sudden sunlight blinded them momentarily, and the staggering heat hit them full force.

Major Entebe continued past a set of cones and stepped over a rope line, heading toward a twin engine Turbo Commander that was still being fueled. "Lieutenant Fatima just flew back from Lagos this morning and took a coastal route that we will mirror at a lower altitude. He told me that he was too high up to find the camp we are looking for, but he thinks that there are some promising areas we should check out," he explained.

Lieutenant Fatima was already in the cockpit going through his checklist prior to their flight.

"At least this plane is a little bigger than I thought it would be. I am not a fan of small planes," Hans said pointedly, shaking his head.

The pilot noticed the group heading toward his aircraft and got up from the cockpit to greet them.

"You are welcome," Lieutenant Fatima said as they all met at the door of the aircraft. "I will be flying without a copilot this afternoon, so if someone would like to sit in the right-hand seat, that will be permitted—but hopefully it's someone with at least a little bit of flight experience."

"I flew Cessna 172s with my dad," Morgan said as she stepped forward, anxious to sit in the cockpit, but then looked to the others in the group for their permission.

"That will be fine. I will be in the jump seat behind you. George and Hans can look out the side windows," Major Entebe directed.

"There are headsets for everyone in the overhead compartments. Please make sure that they are working before we depart, since I will not be able to help you with them after we take off," the pilot requested.

"Sounds good. Let's get on with this," George said as he climbed into the plane, the others following close behind him.

In less than fifteen minutes, the aircraft and its passengers were ready to depart. The pilot contacted the tower, and number three was cleared for takeoff, despite how busy the airport appeared.

The pilot taxied the Turbo Commander and got in line on the taxiway behind an ancient DC-3 and a 727. Morgan looked over at the young lieutenant at the flight controls and noticed the telltale head bob of a man drifting off to sleep.

"Hey, Lieutenant Fatima, do you need some coffee?" Morgan asked.

"No, thank you, but pass me that water bottle, and I'll take a couple of go pills," the lieutenant replied as he reached into his flight suit and pulled out a small bottle of pills.

"How long have you been up?" Morgan asked with some concern.

"I had a 0600 flight from Port Harcourt to Lagos this morning, so I was up at 0200," the pilot explained.

"Here's the water," Morgan said as she passed the pilot the water bottle and then watched him down two little blue pills with a gulp of water.

In a few more minutes, it was their turn for takeoff, and the Turbo Commander climbed nimbly with only five on board. As they rose to six thousand feet, Morgan was surprised by how far Port Harcourt was from the coast. The landscape below looked like fingers on a hand stretching inland. Most of the estuaries and rivers meandered in a north-to-south orientation, and it became clear why there were almost no east-to-west roads in this part of Nigeria.

"We're looking for an oil rig near a large camp along the river. There should be some vehicles too but no roads into the camp—they were all brought in by barge, according to Tanya and Gwen," George said over the intercom.

"Those rigs are big; that should make things a lot easier. Wow, look at how many there are off the coast," Hans said as he stared out the window on the port side of the aircraft.

"It may be trickier than you think, if it is an old, rusted rig. It may blend into the muddy riverbanks and be hard to see," Major Entebe cautioned.

"I am going to fly parallel to the coast, about ten kilometers inland. It is my guess that they cannot get an oil rig more than fifteen kilometers upriver," Lieutenant Fatima announced.

Morgan picked up a set of binoculars in the cockpit and started conducting a systematic survey back and forth along the riverbanks as the aircraft flew west at approximately 260 knots.

"5NSSB, you have helicopter traffic southbound at five thousand feet," Port Harcourt Tower warned the pilot.

"Port Harcourt Tower, 5NSSB, traffic in sight," the pilot replied as he pointed out two oil company helicopters heading south into the Gulf of Guinea en route to oil rigs on a supply run.

"Wow, they were close," Morgan exclaimed as the two helicopters flew across their flight path just a thousand feet below.

"That was not that close. We are lucky that the tower called us too. Those helicopters fly wherever they want and often do not follow normal flight procedures. I have had close calls more than once because of them," Lieutenant Fatima said with disgust.

After continuing west for another twenty minutes without seeing anything unusual, George's voice boomed over the intercom. "According to this map, we're almost over Okumbiri, and it looks like there are some camps along the riverbank just to the west."

"Yes, I see," the pilot replied as he banked right to get them a bit closer to Okumbiri.

"I see seven barges along a dock but no oil rig," Morgan said as she peered through the binoculars before switching to the camera to snap a few pictures.

"We will fly west for another thirty minutes and then fly back to Port Harcourt a little farther inland," the pilot said with a sleepy-sounding voice, despite the go pills.

The thirty minutes passed with only a few suspicious sightings. Smugglers and isolated villages were strewn across what seemed to be a vast mangrove wasteland. The pilot turned back toward Port Harcourt, this time flying north of Okumbiri. When they were just west of the town, everyone scanned the banks of the river and its tributaries, but there was still no sign of an oil rig.

After another fifteen minutes had passed with no promising sightings, Morgan's cell phone rang. "I guess we're close enough to Port Harcourt for cell service now," she said before answering.

"Morgan, this is Jorge. I think the boys found something," Jorge said excitedly.

"We're in the air on the way back to Port Harcourt now," Morgan replied.

"The boys set up some search criteria and came up with an old oil rig on the opposite side of a set of docks with a bunch of barges and at least an acre of oil drums behind a fence. There's a pretty good-sized camp with at least twelve structures. It's just west of a place listed on the map as Obogoro."

"OK, I'm looking at a map right now, and Obogoro is slightly north of Okumbiri. We just flew over that place and saw barges and a camp but no oil rig or barrels."

"Morgan, remember that the stuff the boys found online is weeks or even months old. But that might be to our advantage. I can try and send a picture to your phone," Jorge offered.

"I can't send or receive pictures, just calls and texts, and I'm lucky to have phone service at all at the moment," Morgan replied.

"I understand. The field with the barrels is about two and a half miles from the docks with the barges. The oil rig is about three hundred meters across the estuary from the harbor."

"OK, Jorge. I'm starting to lose you. We'll give it another try," Morgan said, ending the call.

"Jorge's boys came up with something. They found the barges that we saw west of Okumbiri and saw at least an acre of oil drums and an oil rig just across from the barges," Morgan announced to everyone over the intercom.

"Lieutenant, let's go back and fly lower this time," Major Entebe instructed.

The young pilot shook his head, disappointed, but put the aircraft into a banked descent, pointing the nose of the aircraft toward Okumbiri.

"What if they dismantled the oil rig or moved it after Gwen and Tanya were rescued?" Morgan asked. "Jorge mentioned that the imagery his boys got off the Internet is weeks or even months old."

"Maybe, but that would be one hell of a job to dismantle one of those things. If they were selling it for salvage, I think they would have towed it close to a shipyard," George replied, puzzled.

The aircraft was now at approximately three thousand feet above ground level, and Morgan could see the barges docked side by side; at this altitude, she could also see that six of them were loaded with oil drums. Across the estuary from the barges was a pile of twisted metal wreckage.

"That's the oil rig!" Morgan yelled over the intercom. She took pictures of the wreckage and the barges.

"Bingo! I think we found them. Look at all of those guys running around with guns down there," Hans said in wonder.

"I just hope that we didn't tip them off," Morgan answered worriedly.

"I think that we were high enough the first time we passed over that they may not have noticed us. Even if they did, I doubt that they can be sure that we're the same aircraft coming back for another look," George comforted her.

"I will contact the Nigerian army, and the Nigerian navy will hit the camp, but I am afraid that they will not be able to mount an operation until at least tomorrow morning. This is a very isolated area," Major Entebe said as he switched the radio to a military frequency and contacted the military when he finally found an operational frequency.

"All right then. Straight back to Port Harcourt. They will no doubt be asking me to fly more in the morning, but it should be rather interesting," Lieutenant Fatima said with an enthusiastic smile.

CHAPTER 21

DELTA STATE, NIGERIA
17 2200 JULY

Jim was back in the kennel. There was no food for dinner, so he guessed that he had reached the end of his usefulness and would soon be found as a corpse in the wreckage of a poisoned oil well. He remembered how his German shepherd Mosby had systematically disconnected the chain-link fence of a kennel from its mountings after suffering too many days with the sitters while Jim and his family were on vacation at Disney World. Jim's teeth weren't up to the job, but his belt buckle had some sharp corners, so he stuck the corner of the buckle between the bent loop of a tie wire and twisted. After several attempts, the tie wire that attached the chain mesh to the post was unfastened. The fence was meant to contain police dogs, so there were tie wires after every three links. Jim would need to repeat the process at least six or seven more times—without being seen—to create enough slack in the mesh above the bottom stringer to squeeze underneath and escape.

Jim used the filthy wet mattress to hide his slow progress. He lay on top of the mattress and left a gap between it and the fence that allowed him to continue his work unseen.

Jim twisted through another one of the metal ties, and the belt buckle slipped, digging into his hand and almost prompting him to yell out. Distracted by the pain, he failed to notice the African man who had appeared silently and was now standing above him beside the fence. Jim was startled and realized that he had been caught in the act.

"That is very clever, but you will not hurt your hands if you use these instead," the man whispered as he knelt down next to Jim and clipped the three remaining ties with sturdy wire cutters. "I will help you get out of here if you promise to help me stop Johnathan's insane plan."

"OK. Who are you?" Jim whispered back before he crawled under the gap in the fence while the man stretched it upward with all of his might.

"My name is Midella. I came with Johnathan from the north and have known him since we were children—but his plan is crazy. If he shuts off the oil, there will be a famine in Nigeria worse than what happened in the Biafran war. Nigeria is Africa's most populous country, and you can see that this land is not for agriculture."

"I agree that he has to be stopped. What do you have in mind?" Jim asked skeptically.

"We need to sink the barges with the *inhenishta* and then go to Okumbiri and call the army," Midella responded.

Jim swiftly followed Midella into the mangroves and away from the kennel and then stopped to see whether they had been noticed moving across the lighted compound.

"If we sink the barges and the *inhenishta* goes into the water, aren't we doing his job for him?" Jim asked.

"No, it is not the same as putting it in a well, since there is sunlight. The sunlight kills the organisms in the *inhenishta* after three or four days. In a well, the *inhenishta* continues to grow and spread, consuming the oil."

"Those barges are big. We can't just shoot a few holes in their sides as we run away. Do you have any explosives?" Jim asked, remembering the satchel charges that Johnathan's men had used to destroy the oil rig.

"No, the explosives are too heavily guarded, but there is a way to scuttle them. If we sink them at the docks, the motors and pumps will take days to repair, and that will give the army time to respond. They will believe you. They will just throw me in jail, since they know I am Johnathan's classmate and friend."

"With the *inhenishta* loaded onto the barges, you can bet that they have guards," Jim whispered to Midella.

"Yes, of course. That is why I decided to seek your help. I saw you break that Russian's shoulder. I was one of the cameramen."

"That's why you look familiar," Jim said with a smile. "Do you have any weapons? A knife or a machete?"

"They have machetes in the garden shed. It is on the way to the docks, but we need to stay in the mangroves and move around the camp, or we will be detected."

"They don't guard the mangroves?" Jim asked.

"There is no need. That area is full of deadly snakes and croco-diles," Midella said in a somber tone.

Jim remembered his days in the Florida Everglades. The man-groves there were tough going, but it was a broken ankle, not a snake or a crocodile, that you needed to worry about the most while moving through them. Jim also tried to remember the different types of mangroves. There were red, black, and white ones, and you could tell how close to the coast you were depending on the spe-cies you saw. The white mangroves were closest to the ocean. Jim remembered that because salt was white and the ocean was salty. These were red mangroves, not black, and Jim couldn't recall at the moment which meant what.

"Midella, we're dead anyway, so let's die trying. Lead the way until we get those machetes. If you are seen, just make up some dumb-ass excuse, and I'll take out whoever stops you, OK?" Jim instructed him.

Midella nodded his head in agreement and nimbly climbed through the tangled roots of the mangroves, staying about fifty meters away from the cleared area around the camp. Two Russian guards smoking cigarettes walked by with their AKMs shouldered, which let Jim know that his escape had not yet been discovered. He considered taking out the two Russians and tak-ing their weapons, but without having even a knife, that would be too risky. Those Spetsnaz guys were not exactly staying in shape out here in the middle of Nigeria, but they did know how to fight.

When the two Russians were past them, Midella sped up. Except for making a couple of splashes as he slipped off a root, he surprised Jim by how quietly he moved. Up ahead, there was a garden shed near the edge of the mangroves. It was dimly lit, but anyone in the camp looking in their direction would see them. Jim caught up with Midella so that they could communicate.

"I will sneak up and get a couple of machetes. If anyone sees you, the alarm will go out immediately," Midella whispered.

Jim nodded in agreement and lay down on his belly in the grass between the mangroves and the shed to watch Midella's escapade.

Midella calmly walked to the shed, not wanting to look out of place in case he was seen, and opened the door. There was a flash-light on inside the shed, and Jim heard a Russian yell for Midella to go away. Jim jumped to his feet and sprinted the twenty meters to the shed. A Russian guard had Midella pinned to the wall by his throat, and a naked African teenage girl was cowering in the corner, attempting to cover herself with a blanket.

The Russian turned and saw Jim just as Jim swung his leather belt over the Russian's head and wrapped it around his neck, chok-ing him. As the Russian released his grip on Midella's neck, Midella violently and repeatedly kneed the Russian in the groin while Jim continued to choke the man into unconsciousness.

The girl stood up, wrapped in the blanket; Jim blocked the door, expecting her to bolt out, but instead, she hurried toward her clothing. She picked up an open bottle of vodka sitting next to her clothes and took a big swig and immediately spewed the vodka on the floor. On the second swig, she swished her mouth before spew-ing the vodka on the now dead Russian. Midella motioned for her to remain silent, and Jim stepped forward, ready to place a hand over the frightened girl's mouth.

"At least we now have an AKM and some machetes, but what do we do about her?" Jim asked, pointing at the girl.

"I don't know her. We may need to—" Midella started before Jim interrupted him.

"We aren't gonna kill an innocent girl to increase our chances of survival," Jim said evenly as he stared straight into Midella's eyes.

"You are right. As you said, we are already dead," Midella replied with a meek smile.

"Do you want to come with us and get out of here?" Jim asked the girl.

"Yes. I came to cook. They rape me almost every day. There is no escape," the girl said without emotion.

"You're a tough young lady. You can come with us, but you need to be quiet, understand? My name is Jim. What's your name?" Jim asked patiently.

"My name is Fiona," she said more forcefully. "I trust you, Jim. You killed him," she added as she kicked the dead Russian in the face.

"Midella, I want you to walk hand in hand with her. If you're stopped, all they will suspect is that you're trying to get some private time with this beautiful young woman. Are you OK with that, Fiona?"

"Yes, I understand. I will make it look like he is my boyfriend." as she quickly finished dressing.

"That's perfect. I'll be following close behind. If I need to use the gun, we may not get out of here, so try to be calm no matter what happens. OK?" Jim asked.

"Yes, of course. Let's go now," Fiona said, tugging on Midella's hand.

The three moved back into the mangroves and attempted to parallel the road to the docks. Fiona struggled to keep up as she had never ventured into a mangrove swamp before. There was more than a mile left to go when Jim stopped Midella.

"We're not going to make it before dawn at this rate," Jim warned the other man.

"Yes, you are correct. We need to take the road. Can you keep up with us in the mangroves?" Midella asked warily.

"Yes, I have to," Jim answered, determination set on his face. "Try to walk quietly, and expect to be stopped. When they stop you, act innocent, and offer to go back to the camp. Keep them engaged, and I will try to fix things. Midella, you take one of the machetes and put it in your belt like that's a normal thing. Don't try to hide it, or the guards will suspect that something is up."

"OK. Fiona, are you OK?" Midella asked.

"Yes. Let's go. I want out of here," Fiona whispered.

Midella and Fiona were making good time on the road, but Jim was taking a beating trying to keep up with them while staying hidden in the mangroves. His shins were bloody from scraping them on the slippery mangrove roots and falling into the holes in the muck.

It took almost a half hour to cover the last mile, and as the road opened up to the cleared area around the docks, a Russian guard stepped forward and challenged Midella and Fiona. "Stoy, halt, stop! Hey, where the hell do you two think you are going?" the sentry barked.

"We wanted to take a walk to get away from the camp. I am Johnathan's cinematographer," Midella said honestly.

"Oh, you. I know who you are, but you are not supposed to be here. Especially not tonight. Don't you know what we are doing in the morning?" the Russian asked.

"Of course. That is why I need to spend time with Fiona. It may be our last chance to—"

Midella almost vomited when Jim's machete sliced halfway through the Russian sentry's neck, killing him instantly and spurting blood from his severed jugular vein like a fountain.

"I thought that only happened in anime," Midella said, as he finally did throw up onto the road.

Fiona patted Midella on the back and whispered in his ear, "This nightmare is almost over."

Jim collected the Scorpion submachine gun from the sentry and handed the AKM he had been carrying to Midella along with the two magazines that he had grabbed from the rapist in the garden shed. "All right, Midella, you know how to scuttle these barges, so get to it. Fiona and I will get one of the powerboats ready to go," Jim ordered.

"There is another guard by the dock," Midella whispered.

"Let me go. I know what that Russian wants. Just don't take too long killing him, OK?"

Midella looked at Jim inquiringly. Jim nodded his head and got into position behind one of the pilings to use the Scorpion if it was needed. Fiona stepped onto the dock.

"Stoy! Stay there," the Russian ordered.

"It's Fiona. I missed you so much after last week that I had to come see you."

"Really? I, uh, didn't know you liked me..."

"After what you did, I want it again and again," Fiona pleaded sweetly.

The sentry unzipped his pants and pulled out his cock. "You are a wonderful African princess," he said as Fiona moved closer.

The Russian placed his AKM on the dock and put his hands around Fiona's head, pulling her face closer to his body. He felt her mouth on his cock and then the strange sensation of something sharp pushing up into his chest from underneath his ribs before he lost consciousness.

Midella hurried onto the dock. "Where did you get the knife?" he asked with a very worried look.

"From the other dead Russian. Now finish what you need to do with these boats so we can leave," Fiona ordered.

Midella looked around and made sure that there were no other sentries on the docks. He then ran onto the first barge, pulled up a hatch near its stern, and disappeared into the hull. In less than five minutes, Midella emerged and gently lowered the hatch door before dancing across the deck onto the next barge. As Midella disappeared into the hull of the second barge, Jim stood guard. He noticed that the first one had already started to sink.

Fiona was still staring at the Russian sentry she had killed, and Jim understood what she was going through. He moved onto the dock and motioned for Fiona to follow him. He put his arm around her shoulder. "This is what makes us human," Jim whispered into her ear. "No matter what he did, this is not easy for us, and I understand."

Fiona hugged Jim around the middle. "Thank you. We must go soon!" she urged insistently.

"I have some bad news: the powerboats don't have fuel cans connected, and I can't find any on the dock. The good news is that I cut the fuel hose connectors off every boat except for the one we're going to take," Jim said.

"How will we get away from here?" Fiona asked in a panicked tone.

"We paddle, and we'll have a head start," Jim answered with an encouraging smile.

"Why not take the barge?" Fiona asked.

"We are more likely to get it stuck, since we don't know this channel, but I guess we can tow the small boat and start paddling if we do get stuck. If we can get one started," Jim replied. He moved across the dock to intercept Midella, who was just emerging from the hull of the fifth barge.

"Midella, can we get one of these started?" Jim asked in a loud whisper.

"I think so, but I don't know how to drive one. We have barge captains for that," Midella explained.

"I might be able to do it; if not, we paddle the rest of the way, and if we block the channel and slow down Johnathan's men, all the better. Fiona and I will pull the small boat around the other barges and tie it off to this one so that we can tow it along," Jim said as he pointed at the sixth barge.

"You need to hurry, Mr. Jim. When I start the barge, anyone near us will wake up and figure out that something is wrong," Midella said with a concerned look on his face.

"Yeah, I thought about that, but someone might sound the alarm any moment anyhow with the dead Russians that we left in our wake," Jim replied. He motioned for Fiona to follow him, and they briskly walked down the dock to retrieve the small boat.

Jim and Fiona untied the boat and started making their way around the other barges. They dragged the boat forward and then jumped to the next barge before pulling the boat forward again, and by the time they were on the third barge, Fiona's arms had given out, and Jim realized that he was doing the majority of the pulling.

"Fiona, go help Midella. I've got this," Jim said encouragingly.

Fiona skipped across the next two barges and joined Midella in the wheelhouse of the sixth as Jim tugged with all of his might to pull the boat against the current, which seemed to be getting stronger by the minute. *It must be the tide going out,* Jim thought as he reached the sixth barge and tied the boat off on one of the cleats at its stern. He heard the starting sequence of the barge's big diesel engine begin, and the powerful motor sputtered to life, belching stinky black diesel smoke.

On the other side of the harbor, lights came on in what may have been the guardhouse.

"Come on! We've got to go," Jim yelled to Midella over the roar of the diesel engine. "Help me with the lines."

Jim pulled the bowline off the barge and threw it onto the deck, but the current was now gripping the barge, and the stern line was too taut to pull off the cleat.

"Can you back up a bit and take tension off the line?" Jim yelled again.

Midella looked at the controls and pulled on a lever, which made the engine roar louder for a moment, but the barge did not budge.

"Never mind," Jim said as he pulled out his machete and chopped at the four-inch-thick hemp line. He chopped hard with the machete, but the thick line held; luckily, the weight of the barge stretched open the cut he had made in the line, giving Jim a target for the next chop. On the third chop, the line snapped free, and the barge began to drift from the dock as Jim jumped on board.

Men backlit by the lights in the guardhouse were now pointing at the barge and waving their arms excitedly. Jim saw the silhouette of AKM assault rifles as two more men emerged from the building and started to run toward the docks.

Jim moved into the wheelhouse and shoved Midella and Fiona out of the way as he moved in front of the controls. "Two guards with AKMs are headed this way. Don't let them get on board," he instructed Midella. "Fiona, you stay low."

Jim looked at the controls and was relieved to see that they were not that different from the controls on the small boats he had grown up around as a kid in Miami. He pushed the transmission lever forward and felt the boat shudder and the engine's rpm decline. He added throttle, and the boat slowly began to accelerate away from the dock, heavy from the full barrels lashed to the deck.

Jim spun the wheel to turn the barge out into deeper water but overdid the turn a bit, so the right side of the barge scraped one of the pilings at the end of the dock, producing a screeching metallic howl as the boat dragged along the dock and slowed until its stern had passed the wooden obstacle.

Jim's concentration on piloting the barge was suddenly interrupted when gunfire erupted from the dock behind them, and the sound of the bullets striking the metal barge prompted him to duck. Almost immediately, Midella returned fire with his AKM, firing full automatic and expending a full magazine, much to Jim's dismay.

Jim grabbed the other AKM and fired through the wheelhouse window, aiming for the muzzle flashes on the dock; he fired two-shot bursts three times in rapid succession. The firing from the dock finally ceased, so Jim turned his attention back to piloting the barge. He immediately noticed that he was headed directly for the far bank and corrected the course before he ran them all aground.

"Fiona, please check on Midella," Jim said after realizing that Midella had stopped firing but had not returned to the wheelhouse.

Fiona ran back to where Midella had been firing from.

Jim looked out front again and recognized that it was starting to get light. He could see bullet holes in the walls of the wheelhouse from shots that must have missed him by inches. He was just getting over his amazement when Fiona called out from behind the wheelhouse.

"Mr. Jim! Come quick!"

Jim checked their course and guessed that he could be away from the wheel for a minute or two. He ran back to where Fiona had called from and saw Midella lying in a pool of blood, bleeding badly from a bullet wound in his lower leg. Jim bent down to take a look at the leg. He pulled Midella's pants leg up and saw that fragments of shattered bone were protruding from the wound, which was sending Midella into shock.

"Fiona, please run back to the wheelhouse and try to keep us in the middle of the channel. I have to stop this bleeding," Jim said as he ripped off his shirt without taking the time to unbutton it. "You are gonna be OK, Midella," Jim reassured the shivering man.

DELTA STATE, NIGERIA 17 2200 JULY

Jim wadded his T-shirt and placed the cloth over the gushing wound. Midella grimaced as Jim moved his leg and used the long sleeves of the button-down to tie a pressure bandage.

"Fiona, bring me three life jackets from the cabinet in there," Jim yelled.

In moments, Fiona arrived with the life jackets. Jim flattened one out and placed it under Midella's head for comfort before stacking the other two life jackets under Midella's legs to slow the bleeding and get more of Midella's remaining blood to his vital organs. He checked the wound again and was satisfied that the bleeding had mostly been arrested.

"You are gonna make it, buddy," Jim said to Midella as he put a hand on his shoulder.

Fiona rushed over with a water bottle that she had found in the wheelhouse and knelt down to give Midella some water.

"Just a few sips at a time, OK?" Jim instructed her.

Fiona nodded, and Jim rushed back to the wheelhouse. He adjusted their course and looked back to make sure that no one was chasing them from the docks.

A sudden change in the sound of the motor startled Jim. A slight bow-to-stern rocking started up just as trails of mud appeared behind the barge. The light was shifting from twilight to dawn, so Jim could now see that the stern of the barge was beginning to sink lower in the water. He quickly ducked below deck and realized what had happened. Apparently, a bolt on the pilling they had scraped against had gouged a foot-long gash in the side of the barge, and the stern had dropped faster the more water had poured in. They were definitely sinking.

Jim jumped back in front of the controls, pushed the throttle forward, and steered toward a sandbar near a curve in the channel. The propellers of the boat caught more mud, and the diesel engine labored before a loud bang and clanking sound came from below. The engine roared as the rpm suddenly increased.

Realizing that the barge had broken a propeller shaft, Jim shut off the engine. He looked at the map, and it looked like Okumbiri was just around the bend they were approaching. As the barge continued to move forward from momentum and the current, Jim was satisfied that they would make it to the sandbar before they sank. He ran back to Midella and Fiona.

Midella was conscious now, and Fiona was holding his hand and rubbing gently on his head. "What is happening, Jim?" Midella asked with a grimace.

"We put a hole in the side when we hit the dock, and we've started to sink. We're going to run aground on a sandbar any minute now, so hold on," Jim warned just seconds before the three were thrown forward and the barge spun forty-five degrees before coming to rest on the sandbar.

The jolt forward had shifted Midella's position, so Jim quickly checked Midella's leg, tightening the bandage around it.

"We are going to try to get you into the small boat. There's a village just around the bend, and they probably have some medical supplies. I'll pull the boat around to this side of the barge so that we won't need to move you far," Jim said as he ran back to grab the line tied off on the stern of the barge.

Jim had just bent over to untie the boat when he heard a motor and looked up the channel. Two boats were headed their way at high speed. He knew that they would be loaded with killers, and he didn't have very much ammunition left to stop them. He rushed back to Midella and Fiona.

"They are coming fast, and we are going to have to move you," Jim said as he bent down and began to lift Midella by his shoulders to drag him backward.

"Ahhhh!" Midella yelled out, prompting Jim to stop. "I can walk on one leg if you can help me up," the African man grimaced.

Jim pulled Midella to his feet, and the two made it into the wheelhouse with Fiona getting to work immediately in her hurry to situate Midella with his leg up.

"Midella, how do you work the high-pressure sprayer?" Jim asked.

"It runs from the main motor. The controls are just an on/off lever and triggers on the handle. It was adapted from a sprayer on a fire department boat," Midella explained.

"I have an idea—I just hope that we didn't take on too much water to get the motor started," Jim said as he pushed the button to crank the diesel engine. The barge sprang to life after only a few seconds, and smiles appeared on the faces of Midella and Fiona.

The boats were getting closer, and soon they slowed, wary of approaching the grounded barge. Four armed men were on each of the two boats.

"OK, when they are almost here, we fire at them to get their heads down, and I'll spray them and sink their boats. I saw the navy do that once to keep rioters from getting on board," Jim said.

"That was water though. The *inhenishta* will do horrible things to them. It will blind them almost instantly. We had some accidents when we were testing the clamp that holds the pressure nozzle onto the well pipes," Midella warned.

"I hate to say this, but that's even better. We might have a chance. These guys are pretty good shots, and we don't have much ammo left," Jim said grimly as he hurried over to the spray gun and hid behind the pedestal where it was mounted.

The sandbar prevented the attackers' boats from approaching them on two sides, or else the plan would have had little chance of success. It was still risky, since as soon as Jim started to spray, the attackers would probably focus their fire on him.

Jim peeked out from his hiding place and wasn't surprised to see that one of the boats was headed toward the stern while the other one hung back a bit just off the port side of the barge. Jim judged that the farther boat was just coming into range of the pressure gun. He jumped up, flipped the lever, pointed the improvised water cannon at the boat, and pulled the trigger, not knowing what to expect. The stream was narrower than Jim had expected, but it was under such high pressure that it knocked one gunman over the side of the boat. As Jim directed the stream into the boat, instead of filling and sinking it as Jim had expected, the stream burst through the far side of the boat and nearly ripped the fiberglass hull in two.

Two Russians and one African were just climbing off their boat onto the stern of the barge while another African man remained at the controls of the boat. They looked stunned when their comrade's boat sank in seconds and were still watching the spectacle when Fiona fired Midella's AKM through the window of the wheelhouse, not hitting any of the attackers but distracting them. Jim was able to turn the deadly stream on the three attackers on deck. The men screamed and reached for their faces before they were swept off the deck. The remaining man in the boat had had enough; he pushed the throttle forward, turned the boat, and raced back upriver, not even stopping to help his now blind comrades who were thrashing in the water.

Jim climbed down from the pressure gun and headed to the wheelhouse. Fiona rushed past him, and before Jim could stop her, she emptied their last AKM magazine into the two Russians thrashing in the water closest to the boat. Jim understood her rage after what she had been through but almost chastised her before thinking better of it.

Fiona threw the empty AKM onto the deck. Jim still had the Scorpion and two magazines, but that was it, and he knew that more attackers would follow after they had repaired more of the boats.

"Midella, these guys will be back as soon as they fix another boat. We can't move you now. You'll need to convince Johnathan that I kidnapped you, OK?"

"Yes, that is what I was thinking too. The village is not far. You and Fiona can make it there on foot. I need you to take something though," Midella finished as he unbuttoned a shirt pocket and pulled out an SD card. "This is the film of the trial run on the oil rig. You must show it to the authorities," he insisted.

Jim reached up for his shirt pocket and realized that he was missing his button-down after having used it for a bandage. He stuck the card in his pants pocket and got Midella another bottle of water.

"I wonder whether there are crocodiles here," Jim mused as he looked for the best path to shore.

"There are none here, or they would be eating the Russians," Fiona said wisely.

Jim smiled and checked the bandage on Midella's leg one last time.

"Listen!" Fiona yelled suddenly.

The sound of boat motors was getting closer, and this time, there were more than two. Jim hurried back to the pressure gun, planning on making a last stand; he moved the lever forward and aimed upriver. The sound of the boat motors grew louder, and Jim strained his eyes, expecting to see more attackers any second. Instead, as river patrol boats emerged from around the bend downriver, Jim laughed with relief.

"Fiona, Midella, it's the cavalry," Jim joked.

"Cavalry?" Fiona said with a very confused look.

"It's an American saying from the Old West. The Nigerian navy is here!" Jim exclaimed gleefully as one of the patrol boats pulled up next to the barge and boarded with weapons ready.

Jim raised his hands in the air. "I'm an American," he yelled out. "The bad guys went upriver. We have a wounded man in the wheelhouse."

Nigerian marines moved across the boat and into the wheelhouse. They pushed Jim to the ground, pulled his machete out of its sheath, cut the strap of the Scorpion, and pulled the gun away from him before giving him a full pat-down search.

A second boat pulled up, and George West jumped onto the barge with a Nigerian marine captain and headed over to Jim. "That's Jim Stillwater. Let him up," George barked.

"He had many weapons," a marine sergeant said, pointing at the machete and Scorpion submachine gun.

"The man who helped me escape has a bullet wound to the leg. He needs medical attention. The woman, Fiona, was one of their hostages," Jim yelled as he got to his feet.

"What's the situation, Stillwater?" George asked.

"A nutcase named Johnathan is trying to establish a caliphate with the help of the Russians. They were planning to contaminate the oil field by injecting the shit in those barrels into the wells. The Russians have Spetsnaz helping these guys."

"How far upriver?" the Nigerian marine captain asked.

"Just a couple of miles. We disabled their boats, but they fixed some of them and came after us, thus the floating Russians."

"Are there any innocents in the camp?" the captain asked.

"There are some. The cooks and workers and a few hostages, so maybe fifteen or twenty. There are at least forty armed men, mostly Russians but some Africans too," Jim explained.

Two medics hauled Midella out of the wheelhouse on a stretcher with Fiona following close behind. When she saw Jim, she ran over and hugged him. "Thank you, Mr. Jim," she said through tears.

Jim hugged her back and held her at arm's length by the shoulders for a moment. "Make sure they take care of Midella, OK? I'll catch up with you two later."

Fiona nodded, turned, and raced after Midella, who was being lifted onto the patrol boat.

"So, you know what he looks like? You feel good enough to come along?" George asked hopefully but reluctantly.

"If I can take those," Jim said as he pointed at the submachine gun and the machete before swatting another mosquito that had landed on his bare chest.

"How about a shirt too? I have a T-shirt on under this," George said as he pulled off his polo shirt and handed it to Jim.

Jim smiled, pulled on the shirt, and picked up the machete and the submachine gun. "Let's do this."

"My marines will sweep the area first. We have machine guns on the patrol boats to provide covering fire."

"The main camp is up a jeep trail, more than a mile inland from the docks. Johnathan lives in what must be an old plantation house. It's an old wooden Victorian mansion that has somehow survived the termites," Jim said.

"They made them from cedar," George explained. He addressed the marine captain. "Once you've secured the area, we'll go in after Johnathan."

"That will be acceptable," the captain replied.

"OK, let's go," George said as he led Jim onto the first patrol boat.

There were twenty Nigerian marines—ten on each side in the back of the patrol boat. They looked at Jim curiously as he removed the broken strap from his weapon, since they had cut it in two when they had taken it away from him.

"Hey, do you want something other than that piece of shit?" George offered as he pointed at the Scorpion.

"Wadda yah got?" Jim asked.

"I have an M4, a Glock 9, and a Sig 226 for backup. You want the Glock? I have two spare mags."

"That'll work. I'll keep the Scorpion too," Jim said with a smile as George handed over the Glock.

"I learned to shoot at Bragg too, before I joined the DEA, so we should be able to work together just fine. I read your military file after we worked together back in the day," George said with his own smile.

Their conversation was interrupted when the patrol boat lurched forward and both men had to grab onto railings to stay on their feet.

"Giddy up!" George said with a laugh.

"How's Gwen?" Jim yelled over the roar of the patrol boat.

"She played a big part in finding you. We were looking up north until Gwen recognized a picture of Johnathan on an FBI agent's laptop and told us that he was at the camp where she and Tanya had been held. We never would have found you otherwise," George answered, patting Jim on the back. "You wanna call her?" George held up an Iridium satcom phone.

"Of course I do!" Jim exclaimed.

"I have your wife on speed dial now," George said with a grin as he jabbed his elbow into Jim's ribs and pushed some buttons before handing Jim the phone.

"Hello, George?" Gwen answered.

"*George*? Did you forget my name already?" Jim teased.

"Are you OK?" Gwen responded, flustered. "It was George's number. I—"

"I know. He's right here, and he told me how you got them to look for me in the right place," Jim said proudly. "We're going to take care of Johnathan now. The Nigerian navy rescued me from a barge that two other people and I escaped on. A guy named Midella and a woman named Fiona. They're taking them to Port Harcourt. Midella got shot in the leg."

"Morgan and Hans are in Port Harcourt. The marines wouldn't let them go with George. I'll tell them to find Midella and Fiona and make sure they get taken care of."

The patrol boat slowed, and the big .50-caliber machine gun on the bow boomed to life.

"Hey, I gotta go," Jim said hurriedly.

"I heard that. Go. Be careful," Gwen said before Jim ended the call and handed the phone to George.

"I hope that I didn't run up your bill too much." Jim chuckled.

"One more thing we can blame on Johnathan. I'm gonna be pretty pissed by the time we find him. I had a tee time in Abuja today with the defense attaché," George said truthfully.

The boat suddenly accelerated, made a speedy turn to starboard, and slammed against the dock; rubber bumpers quickly dropped over the side to protect the hull. The .50 caliber boomed to life again, and two more machine guns on other boats joined the cacophony.

The twenty marines let out a simultaneous yell, jumped to their feet, and scrambled onto the dock, rifles at the ready.

There was still light machine gun fire coming from the guard-house that had lit up during Jim's earlier escape, and Jim guessed that the structure must have been sandbagged inside. Two of the marines fell to the dock, hit by the fire, before the 0.50 caliber on the boat blew through whatever had been used for cover in the guardhouse. The building briefly erupted in fire before it disintegrated with a bright flash, sending debris raining down over a fifty-yard radius.

The marines fanned out, with one platoon setting up a perimeter around the harbor. The two remaining platoons formed up and began a bounding overwatch up both sides of the jeep trail leading to the main compound.

Jim and George jumped onto the dock and headed for the jeep trail along with the marine captain and his radio operator. Jim heard an aircraft in the lull in the fighting and saw a Turbo Commander orbiting above.

"We were in that plane yesterday. That's how we found this place," George said when he noticed Jim looking up at the aircraft.

Jim nodded and jogged down the road, moving off to the side, away from the marine captain and his radioman.

"George, don't stay too close to him. Russians, remember?" Jim yelled to George.

George nodded and ran over next to Jim. Not even two seconds later, a single shot rang out, and the marine captain fell to the ground. The radio operator dove down and was hit with a second shot. The entire platoon on the right-hand side of the road went prone and returned fire, apparently aware of where the sniper fire was coming from.

The platoon on the left stood up and ran forward, firing down the road in front of them into possible hiding places. As they emerged into the clearing where the camp was located, the marines detected the Russians withdrawing to the north, heading into the mangrove swamps. They moved quickly from building to building, bringing the remaining inhabitants out and making them sit with their hands on their heads.

The trailing platoon that had eliminated the sniper moved through the camp and set up a defensive perimeter in case the Russians counterattacked.

Jim and George rendered aid to the Nigerian marine captain and his radioman until a medic arrived. It looked like both men would survive. They waved at the medic and jogged down the road behind the second platoon that had entered the camp. Jim pointed the way to the Victorian mansion. A squad of marines surrounded the mansion, and George motioned for them to watch for anyone trying to escape out the back of the building.

"Ready?" Jim asked from the shelter of a large palm tree.

"Yep," George answered just before he waved at the marines to fire at the front of the building to cover their approach to the front porch.

The two Americans moved forward, and before they arrived at the porch, the marines had ceased their fire. George paused to make sure that they were really done and then charged forward with Jim close behind.

"I'll go high, you go low," George said to Jim before he kicked in the front door and cleared the room to the right while Jim entered in a low crouch and made sure that the left was clear. They heard the spoon of a hand grenade bounce against a wall after the pin was pulled, and a grenade bounced its way down the stairs.

Both Jim and George jumped back out through the door and crashed belly first onto the wooden porch just as the grenade exploded in the interior hallway.

George flashed the OK symbol to Jim, who returned it but pointed to his ears, not able to hear anything except for a tone that sounded like the off-the-air tone used in the early days of TV. George gave a thumbs-up, jumped to his feet, and ran back through the door, firing at the top of the stairs.

Jim followed George up the stairs but turned backward and aimed at the balcony above in case someone was waiting to shoot them from behind. Still unable to hear, the two made it to the top of the stairs and looked down the row of doors. Jim pointed at the open door of a dumbwaiter or laundry chute and thought at first that Johnathan had escaped that way after throwing the grenade. A closer look showed that it went to the kitchen below and was not big enough for a grown man to fit inside.

Jim pointed at the master bedroom in the corner of the house, and George gave a thumbs-up in agreement. They paused by the door, and this time, Jim kicked it in, his Glock ready. George was about to move into the room with his M4 when what they saw caused both men to freeze in their tracks. Johnathan was standing on the other side of the room with a suicide vest on. He was plugging the arming device together while the trigger device hung loose at his side.

Without further hesitation, Jim started firing directly at the wiring harness, attempting to sever the safety before Johnathan could reach the trigger button hanging at his side on two feet of wire. George saw what Jim was doing, and as Johnathan reached for the trigger despite having taken more than six rounds of fire into his abdomen, George opened up full automatic into Johnathan's head, sending him careening out the window.

"Wow, that was close!" Jim yelled and wiped perspiration from his forehead.

"I can't hear you," George yelled. "But that was close."

Jim took a step toward the window to look down at Johnathan on the ground below. As he started to take a second step in that direction, a tremendous blast from beneath them knocked Jim and George off their feet, and the outer wall of the building went completely missing.

Jim slowly got to his feet, stumbled over to where the wall had been, and looked over the edge. There was a twenty-foot-wide crater where Johnathan had fallen.

"Wow, that was close!" Jim repeated to George before he sat down, still rocked by the explosion.

George came over and sat down next to Jim after he had stumbled over near the edge and examined the crater for himself. "Wow, that was close," he yelled into Jim's ear.

"That's what I said!" Jim answered, yelling into George's ear.

The two men put their arms over each other's shoulders to keep from falling over and howled at their predicament for a few moments before they struggled back to their feet and headed down the stairs and out of the building onto the front porch. George waved at the marines, who were watching in amazement as the two men emerged from the building.

When George sat down on the stairs, Jim pulled Johnathan's rocking chair over beside him and sat down.

"I could use a gin and tonic about now," Jim said as his hearing slowly started to return.

George reached into his butt pack, pulled out a flask, took a swig from it, and passed it to Jim. "How about Tennessee whiskey instead?" he asked.

"That'll do."

CHAPTER 22

ORLEAN, VA
18 0200 JULY

"What is it, Mosby?" Jorge said to the dog now sitting with his nose inches away from Jorge's face. Mosby's hair was standing up on his back. When he saw that Jorge was awake, the dog raced back down the stairs and resumed his angry barking at the front door.

Jorge got out of bed and pulled the drapes back to peer discreetly through the window of the second-floor guest room out over the long driveway and the stand-alone garage. There was a Dodge Charger with North Carolina license plates parked in the driveway with its motor running. Two military-looking men were pouring gasoline around the walls of the garage where Gwen kept her vintage Shelby Cobra.

Jorge pulled on his sweatpants, grabbed his Glock G30 off the dresser, and went to the second door down the hall, where Miles and Patrick were sleeping. Mosby was now standing by the front door and growling low.

"Boys, wake up. Some bad guys are getting ready to burn the place down. Miles, call 911. Patrick, come downstairs, and when I say 'now,' let Mosby out the front door, and I'll head out the back door," Jorge instructed his sons. "As soon as I'm outside, lock the doors, go get Mr. Stillwater's shotgun from his office, and wait in your room until the police get here. Got it?"

Patrick and Miles both looked frightened, having just gone to sleep less than thirty minutes before, after watching two of Jim's extremely violent movies in a row.

Patrick followed Jorge downstairs and stood by the front door with Mosby, who was becoming even more agitated. Jorge went to the back door, checked his weapon one last time, and said "now" just loud enough for Patrick to hear before he headed out the back door.

Patrick released Mosby, who began barking loudly and headed around the corner of the house toward the men near the garage. The black German shepherd was almost invisible in the dark except for his bright white teeth.

"Oh shit! There weren't supposed to be nobody at home," one man yelled as he ran and got into the passenger seat of the Dodge Charger.

Mosby turned his attention to the other man, who had a gas can. The man tried to splash gasoline on the German shepherd, but if any actually got onto the dog, it only made him angrier, as he went straight for the man's crotch. Mouth open and fangs bared, Mosby latched onto the man's crotch and started to shake his head back and forth. The man dropped the gasoline can and screamed in agony as he fell to the ground.

Jorge came around the back of the house just as Mosby chomped down; he noticed that the man in the car was attempting to slide from the passenger seat into the driver's seat.

Jorge fired the Glock into the engine compartment, hitting the radiator, but the car was still running, and the man inside put the car into gear and floored the accelerator, trying to hit Jorge.

As Jorge jumped out of the way of the car, a shotgun blast rang out, followed by a high-powered rifle shot, and the Charger stopped in its tracks. All of the car lights went dim.

"Dude! You hit the battery! Way to go," Patrick said to Miles and gave his brother a high five.

Jorge rolled back onto his feet. "Boys, if the guy Mosby's holding stands up, shoot him!"

"Got it, Dad," the boys said simultaneously. "Jinx!"

Jorge moved to the car, Glock held out in front of him, and yelled at the man inside. "Get out and get on the ground!"

Instead, the man dived for the glove box, held up a 0.38 special, and fired at Jorge through the window of the car.

Jorge ducked and fired back twice, double tapping the intruder and killing him instantly. He peered into the car and stepped back as the gasoline pooling on the front lawn around the car began to burn.

Jorge turned his attention to the other man; the boys were both pointing guns at him while Mosby stubbornly held him by the crotch.

"Please let me go. There weren't supposed to be no one at home. We didn't want to hurt nobody—our old boss said that some communist was talking shit and needed to be taught a lesson. Please, mister," the man pleaded.

"Listen, you stupid fuck. You just tried to burn down my friends' home. In Japan, arson results in the death penalty. It kinda worked out that way for your crispy-critter friend. Now tell me who you work for, or I tell the dog to bite it off."

Miles and Patrick laughed.

"Last chance!" Jorge warned.

"It's O'Finn. We had bad conduct discharges, and he called us up and said that if we did this, he would get our discharges changed to honorable so we's could get VA benefits."

"You have a phone?" Jorge demanded.

"Yes, but—"

"Throw it to me, and when the cops get here, don't say anything about it, or I will hunt you down and kill you. Got it?"

The man reached into his pocket, which prompted Mosby to growl louder for a moment. The man threw the phone to Jorge as two Fauquier County deputy sheriffs arrived on scene and immediately called for an ambulance and a fire truck. The officers quickly figured out what was going on when they saw Mosby holding the man on the ground and the two boys, both armed, pointing guns at the same man.

"Boys, put the guns down on the ground. We got this now," the first deputy said reassuringly to Miles and Patrick.

Jorge also placed his gun on the ground and stood in the driveway with his hands up. "Thanks for coming so soon," he greeted the officers.

"You a friend of Mr. Stillwater's?" the first deputy asked.

"I'm watching the dog for him while he's out of town."

"I heard his wife got kidnapped by pirates in Africa. Everyone's talkin' about that. Is she OK?"

"She is, and Jim is too—despite being kidnapped himself in the ransom exchange," Jorge responded.

"You can put your hands down, but please don't pick up the gun. Can you call that dog off? Goddamn, that guy's having a worse time than Mr. Stillwater in my book."

"Mosby, come!" Jorge yelled sharply.

Mosby released the man's crotch, ran over to Jorge, and sat down in front of him.

"Well, not to insult you, sir, but if I had any doubts 'bout your story, they're gone now. Goddamn but that dog did a number on him. His fuckin' pants are soaked in blood," the deputy said in disbelief.

The second deputy handcuffed the man and turned to Jorge. "What were they tryin' to do?"

"They were trying to burn down his house—to warn him not to come after the kidnappers," Jorge replied.

"I think they just made things worse. I've talked to Mr. Stillwater before."

"They sure have," Jorge agreed.

CHAPTER 23

PORT HARCOURT, NIGERIA
18 1400 JULY

"Jim, you look like shit," Morgan said candidly as she walked into Jim's hospital room and leaned over the bed to give him a long hug.

"You look stunning, as usual," Jim said as he used the controls on the bed to help him sit up.

"Hey, break it up, you two, or I'm gonna have to call Gwen," Hans teased as he entered the room.

"How's it goin'?" Jim asked with a big smile.

"I heard that you and George were playing with fireworks," Hans joked. "Hey, they found your phone in what was left of Johnathan's house, so I charged it up for you," he added as he handed Jim the phone.

"A text already this morning. That's weird. 'You'll run out of stuff before I run out of men. Back off!'" Jim read the text out loud.

"What's that about? You don't think its O'Finn, do you?" Morgan asked with a concerned look.

"I doubt it, but who knows?" Jim answered just before his phone rang.

"Jim, this is Jorge. I am really sorry, but there's a big burned spot on your front lawn, in the part where you practice golf."

"Don't worry; the grass just went dormant from the heat. It'll come back with a little water after it cools off."

"Ah, no it won't. It's kinda black after a car burned to the ground."

"OK, Jorge, what happened? Start from the beginning, and go slow. The doc says that I have a mild traumatic brain injury, so I'm in the hospital for at least another day of observation."

"Bottom line: General O'Finn sent two losers who used to work for him to burn down your house. The boys and I stopped them, but one of them burned up inside his car on your front lawn."

"Well, thanks for stopping them. Are the boys OK?" Jim asked with deep concern.

"They thought the whole thing was a blast, and they want to get a job like Mr. Stillwater's so that they can do this all the time," Jorge said.

"I'll talk to them when I get back, but in the meantime, thank them for protecting my house."

"Will do, Jim. But I got a phone off one of the men, and O'Finn called them from Nigeria and put them up to this. They were real losers, and it won't be hard for him to find more like them."

"That's just what he said. I got a text this morning saying that I would run out of things before he ran out of people," Jim replied, putting two and two together.

"That sounds like a challenge. You take care of things over there, and take as much time as you need. The boys and I are having quite a vacation here, so don't worry about your place."

"Thanks, man. Gwen will be heading home tomorrow afternoon. I'm glad that you'll be there."

"Aren't you heading back too?"

"Actually, I had planned to go to the Hague and file statements with the World Court. I also have film evidence of what Johnathan was planning to do that I need to present in person. Now it sounds like I have something else to take care of in Nigeria first."

"Let your friends take care of this. I spoke with Tanya just minutes ago, and after hearing what happened here, she told me that she was heading to Abuja tomorrow."

"She didn't tell me that. I guess I'll have some help when I get there."

"She heard that you have a traumatic brain injury from the explosion, and she expects you to go home and take care of yourself, old man," Jorge scolded.

"I am taking care of myself, just not in the way you mean. Anyhow, the doctors said that the TBI is very mild. I was out for only a second or two."

"How is the guy you were with?"

"George is OK. He flew back to Lagos this morning. He was a little bit farther away when the bomb detonated."

"OK, Jim, I'll let you go, and don't you worry about a thing here, OK?"

"Thanks. You and the boys are awesome," Jim said before he ended the call.

"You're not going to Abuja, are you? You know that you can't just whack O'Finn, not even in Nigeria, and especially since he's connected to the president," Morgan warned.

"I'm not going to whack him; I'm going to get him arrested, and I can't think of a nicer place for him to go to jail than in Nigeria. I'll ask Colonel Ademe to meet me in Abuja tomorrow."

"He said that he knew you from back in the day," Hans said.

"Yeah, we worked together very briefly. I do remember him though," Jim said.

"All right, Jim, don't even think that we're going to let you go to Abuja by yourself, especially now. I'll make the arrangements," Morgan volunteered.

"Sounds great. Now help me get out of this place before I really get sick. The hotel will have better food too."

CHAPTER 24

ABUJA, NIGERIA
20 0700 JULY

"Looks like the band is back together. I don't think we've all been in one place since LP got into trouble down in the Keys," Jim said between bites as he devoured a chicken salad sandwich.

"No, I missed that gig," Hans corrected him.

"Yeah, that's right—Jorge was there, not you."

Tanya and Morgan glanced at each other and pursed their lips.

"Jim, why don't you and I hang out under an umbrella at the pool today and let these guys do the running around?" Tanya suggested.

"That's not a bad idea, and I'm sure that Colonel Ademe would be happy to meet you here. You can buy him a drink that way," Morgan suggested.

"All right, I'm gonna surprise you both: that's not a bad idea. I am feeling a little foggy today, but I do need to go to the justice ministry to swear out the warrants against O'Finn. I don't think the president will like the fact that O'Finn intended to facilitate the destruction of the Nigerian oil industry."

"Do we know whether he's even in the country?" Hans asked.

"He's in Abuja, and Colonel Ademe said that triple S won't let O'Finn leave the country if he gets wind of this and shows up at the airport," Morgan said.

"What if the Russians give him asylum?" Tanya asked.

"They won't help him now. They're still trying to explain all those dead Russians from the camp," Jim replied.

"O'Finn is still an American, and he can go to the US embassy," Hans said.

"George is seeking an indictment for conspiracy to commit terrorism, human trafficking, and kidnapping, based on the statements that Johnathan made on the video. I think we have him boxed in, but he has already tried to burn my house down, and I don't think he was making an idle threat about not running out of people," Jim said with some concern.

"This is when things are most dangerous. He still thinks that he can bully his way out of an indictment. Once they're arrested, guys like O'Finn have more things to worry about than wasting resources on revenge," Morgan said as she sipped a tall ice tea.

"All right, it's settled. Jim and Tanya will go to the ministry of justice and then head back here to hang out at the pool. Morgan and I will head to the US embassy and get your replacement passport. I just need that photo, and we'll give statements to the FBI legat for the terrorism charges that they're working on. We'll meet back here for dinner." Hans outlined the plan for the day.

"You ready? No time like the present, Hans," Morgan said as she took one last sip of her ice tea before standing up.

"Let's go," Hans said as he got up and followed Morgan out of the hotel restaurant.

"OK, Jim. I want to go back to my room and brush my teeth. I'm on another floor, so I'll meet you in the lobby in, let's say, fifteen minutes?" Tanya prompted as she stood up.

"Fifteen minutes it is," Jim replied, standing too.

Jim and Tanya headed back to their rooms, with Jim getting off the elevator on the fifth floor and Tanya staying on the elevator for two more floors up. When Jim opened his hotel-room door, he immediately noted that someone had been in his room. The contents of his suitcase were thrown across the room, and his suitcase had been slashed open. He called hotel security to report the break-in. He found the contents of his shaving kit, including his toothbrush, on the bed, so he brushed his teeth and was almost finished when there was a knock on the door.

Jim peered through the peephole expecting to see hotel security, but it was Tanya, so he opened the door.

"It's been twenty-five minutes, and I was worried about you. I know that you're never late," Tanya explained. "I see why now," she added as she looked around the hotel room.

"I know what they were looking for, but it won't do them a lot of good. George already has a copy," Jim said as he pulled the SD card out of his jacket pocket and held it up for Tanya to see.

"Looks like they were in a hurry—or trying to send a message," Tanya said with a frown.

"Both," Jim said before hotel security finally arrived.

The young Nigerian man was dressed in a suit and tie, and Jim noted the shoulder holster under his jacket. "I see there has been a problem here. Oh my. So what was taken?" the security officer asked.

"As far as I can tell, nothing, but my suitcase was damaged," Jim replied.

"This is very suspicious. Perhaps they mistook the room for that of someone involved with drug trafficking, so first, we will get you moved to another room. Also, we have video surveillance of the hallway, so it will not be difficult to find out who entered your room."

"Thank you. I have an appointment to attend and need to leave, but if you can have my things moved to a room on the seventh floor where my friend here is staying, that would be great."

"Sir, I am sure we can accommodate you. My apologies for this incident. When you return from your appointment, please let the front desk know, and I will meet you in the lobby and provide you with an update."

"OK, thanks," Jim said as he led Tanya out of the room.

The trip to the ministry of justice was uneventful apart from having a possible tail, but the driver was good enough that he was more likely to be someone from the US embassy than any bad guy.

Jim signed typed statements that he had provided to the Nigerians after his rescue from the camp. The government officials were extremely courteous to Jim and Tanya, and the whole process took less than an hour.

Back at the hotel, Jim stopped by the front desk to pick up his new room key and asked to speak with security. The new room was on the seventh floor, next door to Tanya's.

The security officer arrived at the front desk just as Colonel Ademe arrived to check in. The colonel looked closely at Jim and then approached him while Jim was still speaking with the young security officer.

"Jim Stillwater?" Colonel Ademe asked when there was a break in the conversation.

"Sam Ademe? Excuse me, Colonel Ademe? You look almost the same!" Jim exclaimed as he shook hands with the colonel.

"Yes, Jim, it's 'Colonel' now but still 'Sam' to you."

"Let me introduce my associate, Dr. Tanya Melnik."

"Very pleased to meet you, Doctor. Jim, I see that you are speaking with the hotel security. Is everything OK?"

"Well, someone ransacked my room and cut open my suitcase," Jim replied.

"That is terrible but probably not unexpected, considering how much trouble some people are in now. Did you sign your statements at justice already?"

"Yes, we just got back from there and were going to find out what security discovered from the video surveillance," Jim said as he turned to the security officer who was standing there patiently, watching the introductions.

"Mr. Stillwater, the video showed a man speaking with the maid who was cleaning the room. As she departed, he entered and closed the door, placing a Do Not Disturb sign on the handle, so the maid never returned to the room and does not know what happened. I spoke to the maid, and she said that she recognized him as a frequent guest, so she was not suspicious."

"Can I see the video, please?" Jim asked politely.

"I am sorry, sir, but that will be impossible. It is strictly against hotel policy."

"Young man, I have full authority over these matters, and we will need to see the video immediately," Colonel Ademe said as he identified himself with his SSS credentials.

The security officer's eye opened wide, and he looked very frightened. "Yes, sir, of course you have that authority. Please follow me, sir," he stuttered before he led the way behind the front desk to a small security office. He typed in his password and clicked through what appeared to be a fairly sophisticated video surveillance system. He clicked to make the video full screen, and they watched the monitor as a well-dressed man approached the maid while she was in Jim's room and spoke with her briefly. When she went to retrieve some pool towels from down the hall, he stepped into the room and placed the Do Not Disturb sign on the door. He departed five minutes later while the maid was cleaning the room next door.

"That's O'Finn!" Tanya exclaimed.

"I guess we shouldn't be surprised that we all ended up in the nicest American-brand hotel in Abuja," Jim said as he shook his head.

"This is outrageous. He must be very desperate to have done that himself. We need to arrest him now," Colonel Ademe declared as he pulled out his phone.

"Can you show us the video of the hallway where his room is located so that we can see whether he's inside?" Jim asked.

"I can do that for the colonel," the security officer proposed.

"Yes, please proceed," Colonel Ademe directed.

In a few clicks, the security officer had switched the view and fast-forwarded the video from the time of the break-in. On the screen, O'Finn returned to his room about five minutes after he had broken into Jim's, departed again, and did not return.

"I will have men here in the hotel in less than an hour. Please continue to observe his room, and call me immediately if he returns," Colonel Ademe said as he handed the security officer his card.

"Yes, sir," the young man replied.

"Jim, this has been a rough day for you. Give me twenty minutes to change into my bathing trunks, and I'll meet you both at the pool bar so that we can talk."

"That sounds great. I've been trying to get this guy to take it easy. He is still beaten up from the bomb blast," Tanya said as she poked Jim in the side.

"Ouch! There's a big bruise there," Jim complained.

"See what I mean?"

"OK, twenty minutes," Jim said as he headed off to his new room with Tanya close behind.

When Jim arrived at the pool, Colonel Ademe was already there in bathing trunks, sandals, and what looked like a very expensive guayabera.

"Jim, you still wear the Hawaiian shirts! Let me see—oh, classic cars and airplanes on this one," the colonel said admiringly.

"And this way, I can say I have a woody," Jim said as he pointed at the Ford woody station wagon on the shirt. "Speaking of that, here comes Tanya," Jim joked, and the colonel turned to look.

Tanya walked across the patio wearing a fluorescent yellow bikini with an open almost-see-through white cover-up that did little to cover her up. "You haven't ordered drinks yet? I hope you weren't waiting on me."

"Tanya, you are rockin' that bikini. What are you doing for workouts now?" Jim asked.

"Just tai chi. I gave up martial arts last year. Too many bruises, and it was starting to take even longer to recover from injuries. Speaking of which, I don't see how you can possibly walk with some of those bruises on your legs," Tanya said with a stern look.

"Jim is a tough man. I learned that many years ago," Colonel Ademe said.

"I know. I trained with him, and we worked undercover together a couple of times. Some might say he's a bit crazy."

"Ah, now I understand what you meant by associate," the colonel addressed Jim. "And you know Morgan and Hans too?" he asked, turning back to Tanya.

"Yes, but I met them through Jim. He seems to have a knack for that."

"Yes, he does. That is why I am here. Morgan called and said she and Hans will arrive within the hour, so we should not get too drunk before they arrive. Perhaps by then we can drink to the arrest of General O'Finn," Colonel Ademe said with a wide smile.

The three ordered drinks and then took a dip in the pool to cool off. The harsh equatorial sun chased them back under the shade of the tiki bar for their ice-filled drinks, which they finished in no time.

"I'll have the same, gin and tonic with lime, for the next round. I'm gonna hit the restroom," Jim announced after finishing his drink. He followed the signs to the poolside restrooms just around the corner from the tiki bar. "The floor's a little slippery," he noted silently as he stepped up to one of the urinals.

"You have a hell of a lot of nerve to stay at the hotel where I'm staying," a booming voice behind him said. Jim heard the man turn the lock on the door of the restroom. "You're a real dumb fuck too, walking around in a hippy-ass Hawaiian shirt and bathing trunks so that I would be sure you weren't armed."

Jim finished taking a piss and turned around to face O'Finn, who was now holding the small switchblade that he had probably used to cut open Jim's suitcase. "Well, speaking of dumb fucks, you were on camera when you broke into my room this morning, and on top of that, you attacked my home and my family," Jim said before he reached into the urinal, grabbed the hockey-puck-size "urinal mint," and threw it at O'Finn's head. He then slid into him with a sliding tackle and knocked the enormous general off his feet, making him hit his head against the tile wall. Jim repeated the head bang with his left hand while he recovered the knife from the floor with his right.

"As I always say, you don't need to carry a weapon, since the bad guys always bring one to the party for you to take," Jim grinned as he got to his feet.

Enraged, the general charged Jim and grabbed for the knife, and he almost had it before Jim ducked and stabbed him in the crotch. O'Finn wasn't done though; he punched Jim hard in the jaw, and Jim reeled back against the wall. The general was just about to charge Jim again when he was struck from behind as the bathroom door was kicked open.

Tanya grabbed O'Finn from behind with a choke hold. O'Finn was a very big man, and he continued to fight despite the choke hold as his face turned red and then purple. Jim stepped forward and was about to stab O'Finn again when an armed Nigerian stepped into the bathroom doorway and yelled, "Triple S! Stop what you are doing and put your hands up, or I will shoot!"

Jim dropped the knife, and Tanya released the general's neck and raised her hands, but instead of raising his hands, the general tried to punch Tanya in the face—which she blocked—and charged at the SSS agent. O'Finn bowled the man over and tried to scramble for the agent's gun before he realized that two more armed agents were waiting just outside the door of the bathroom. At the sight of two more guns pointed at his head, O'Finn surrendered and was handcuffed.

Colonel Ademe strolled over from the tiki bar with a mai tai in hand. "Well, Jim, it looks like you caught him. We can have that celebration drink after all."

"You are going to just love Nigerian prisons," Jim taunted O'Finn, who looked like he was about to explode.

"Jim, Jim, be nice. Besides, after he is done visiting our prisons, I am sure he will have an opportunity to compare them with those in your country on his own." Colonel Ademe laughed and took another sip of his drink. "Captain, take this piece of shit away from here."

"I promise, I was not spying on you while you peed; I was next door using the toilet, and the general has a very loud voice," Tanya teased Jim.

"Thanks for the help," Jim said sincerely. "He is a big guy."

"Yeah, but I bruised my foot kicking in the bathroom door. My boyfriend is going to scold me for getting back into martial arts," Tanya replied with a chuckle.

"That wasn't exactly tai chi," Jim shot back.

Morgan and Hans walked up just as O'Finn was being dragged away, a noticeably wet bloodstain covering his crotch.

Morgan pointed at O'Finn's groin as he went by. "Don't worry, General. You won't need that in solitary," she mocked him.

"Fuck you," O'Finn yelled back.

"Looks like there was some excitement here," Hans proclaimed.

"Of course! Jim Stillwater is here," Colonel Ademe said, producing a deep belly laugh as his second drink began to take hold.

CHAPTER 25

THE HAGUE, THE NETHERLANDS
25 1400 AUGUST

"How did it go, Jim?" Gwen asked him as he walked out of the World Court grand jury proceeding and met Gwen, Tanya, and Morgan in the lobby.

"It went well. In addition to facing indictments in Nigeria and the United States, O'Finn will likely be indicted for supporting international terrorism and crimes against humanity for his destruction of the coral reefs with the *ochistitel*. A fair outcome, if you ask me."

"What happed with Fiona and Midella?" Tanya asked. "I heard that they testified on human trafficking last week."

"They did, and I spoke to both of them yesterday. So, I guess I'll break the news: Midella proposed to Fiona yesterday, and she accepted."

"Nice!" Tanya replied.

"And there's more: Gwen and I are sponsoring Fiona and Midella for visas, and they have both been accepted at George Mason University."

"Wow, that's fantastic!" Morgan said and clapped. "I understand that Fiona is suing O'Finn too?"

"She is. And sadly, O'Finn is also facing a shitload of civil suits from the people his pirates took hostage. He won't have a penny left to his name," Gwen said mockingly.

"No, he won't!" Morgan, Jim, and Tanya answered in unison.

AUTHOR'S NOTE

Oil spills and well leaks are an unfortunate reality of offshore drilling. The oil and gas industry mitigates the environmental damage these events cause with recovery and dispersal. Recovery is done with skimmers and absorbent material while dispersal uses detergents, solvents, and more recently, biological agents. While dispersal prevents the washing ashore of oil into critical habitats, like mangrove swamps, the environmental impact of the oil that falls to the ocean floor is not yet fully understood. Could this contribute to coral bleaching? I don't know, but I did intend to use this work of fiction to highlight the need to protect the world's reefs, which are some of the most beautiful places I have ever visited. I want future generations to have that same privilege.

To the best of my knowledge, biological and chemical dispersants have not been significant factors in the destruction of reefs, but the potential is there. I do know that the threat to the reefs is real. Increasing ocean temperature is believed to be the most significant factor in coral bleaching. Mechanical destruction from anchors, propellers, and divers harvesting coral for commercial use is also an important factor that needs to be limited with both legislation and education.

Lee A. Sweetapple earned a bachelor's degree in politics and public affairs from the University of Miami. In graduate school, he has studied geographic and cartographic science, international law, and international diplomacy. He retired from the US Army Reserve after attaining the rank of lieutenant colonel, and he is currently a colonel in the Commemorative Air Force, where he supports the Red Tail Squadron educational outreach program.

Sweetapple lives in the foothills of the Shenandoah mountain ridge with his wife and two children. He is also the author of *Vette Head's Not Dead*, *Key West Revenge*, *Templar Codes*, and *WASP Sting*.

www.ingramcontent.com/pod-product-compliance
Lightning Source LLC
Chambersburg PA
CBHW050020180626
46810CB00002B/505